Dedication Page

- To Tina, thank you so much for your continuing and unwavering support. I appreciate you so much. I love you my Sugarbooger.
- To all my boys and my sweet baby girl I love you all so much.
- To my parents, I love you both so much and truly appreciate all that you do for us.
- To Grandma Girl, I love you and miss you. Wish you were here to read my books and see the kids growing up.
- To all my friends and family who have shown me so much love and support, I am truly appreciative. Thank You.

Chapter One

Neither Chuck nor Christy knew that the trouble they were already in was about to get a whole lot worse. As they briskly made their way down the street, they left behind everything they once knew. Over the past few days their lives had gone from a fairytale to a complete nightmare. People they knew and loved had either been torn from them, turned on them or stolen from their lives. They knew that if they survived nothing would ever be the same. The most unfortunate part of the current situation was best friends wouldn't be enough to see them through. They had no idea whether the end was near or if this nightmare would last for an eternity.

Chuck and Christy had known each other since sixth grade and had considered themselves to be best friends. For years they had planned on going on a road trip. They always joked about escaping the craziness of life by running away to Mexico. It would either be just the two of them or with a few friends. Both had recently graduated from college, Chuck was 23 and Christy, his partner in crime, was 24. Harper and Gloria, 23 year old twin sisters, had been best friends since the day they were born. Ever since they came home from the hospital, they were inseparable. They had met Christy when they first started going to school, but it wasn't until 2nd grade that the three of them became good friends. Unlike Chuck and Christy, they had been on tons of road trips but something felt different about this one. So, the sisters decided to tag along, just in case anything exciting was to happen. The last minute addition to their group was Chuck's cousin Steven, who was 24. Chuck and Steven had always gotten along growing up. They were as close as brothers and always had a great time whenever they got together. The five of them had often hung out together, going to bars, clubs, concerts, and sporting events. They may not have had the same taste but they always had an epic time together.

Chuck came from a small family, his parents and a younger sister. He wasn't the jock type but he did like to work out and keep in shape. In high school, he mostly kept to himself. His family went from living in a big city to a smaller town where people were much friendlier. He never liked the city, way too much traffic and the people were always so rude. He was happy when they moved. In high school, he excelled in his English class and science classes.

Especially biology. It helped that he made a close friend by the name of Christy. Christy wasn't a popular girl but she knew everyone and had a very select few close friends. She always preferred quality over quantity. She was a great student with great grades and often helped Chuck with his math homework. She was on the diving team and had lettered on both the varsity and junior varsity teams. Chuck was always there at every meet, silently cheering her on. Gloria and Harper, we're twins and best friends of Christy. Initially they were a bit leary of Chuck when he was the new guy in school but over time they all became close friends. They were both on the track and cross country team. They had each set records for fastest runs during their senior year. Steven, however, was the newest member of their group. He and Chuck were cousins. Both 23 but Steven was 5 months older. They were 2 of the 4 male kids on that side of the family and they always had fun and caused some chaos on occasion. When Steven began hanging out with the 4, which was Chuck's idea, he was always the wild card. He talked them into sneaking in the school after it closed for the day to go swimming. They all got busted by the night security guard and their parents gave them hell for it.

They had all been talking about what they wanted to do after graduation and they all agreed that they wanted to take a break from everything. They wanted a chance to just relax and enjoy themselves before they fully joined the adult world. Gloria and Harper talked about going on a cruise since none of them had ever been on one before, but Steven wasn't a fan of the ocean or being so far away from land. Steven had mentioned going over seas to somewhere like Ireland or England. Most of the group had liked the idea but Steven was the only one with an actual passport. Everyone else had the passport card since they never had the opportunity to go anywhere that far. Christy and Chuck brought up the idea of going somewhere like the Florida Keys or Hawaii. After some deliberation, they all agreed to go somewhere tropical with a nice beach, cold drinks and as far as their passport cards would allow them to go.

Chuck had been searching online for a couple of days for island vacations and he was determined to find the perfect place. The first location he checked out was Hawaii but it seemed too touristy and he knew it would be packed with other vacationers. He thought maybe Puerto Rico would be a fun choice but the flights were overpriced and hotels were booked up for the days they had planned. He decided to take a break from the hunt and take a quick nap before meeting up with Christy for lunch. When he woke up from his nap he was goofing around online and was looking up random stuff letting his boredom get away from him. He received a text message from an unknown number. All it was, was a link and the words "Check This Out NOW". Normally he would have just deleted the text but he had a weird feeling so he clicked it. To his shock and amazement, it was the most incredible and perfect place he had ever seen. It had white sandy beaches, crystal clear waters, amazing hotels and a few fancy romantic restaurants. It was almost too good to be true.

When he showed Christy the brochure he requested by email, she immediately fell in love with the island. The island was located about 100 miles south of the Florida Keys, which meant beautiful sunny weather. The brochure also said the island lives up to its name, La Isla de La Noche which translates to The Island of The Night. It had some amazing looking clubs and bars that looked like they would be packed nightly and there was always some sort of activity going on. The island reviews said it had a small population but the tourists loved the little island paradise. Over lunch Chuck and Christy had been messaging the rest of the group in their island vacation chat. After some deliberation and some burgers, it was decided that reservations were to be made ASAP. Chuck set up the reservations at a resort called La Noche. He booked a cozy looking cabin, a rental car and the flights to the island. They planned on having the time of their lives. Little did they know it might just be their last good time together.

Finally, the day came when the five friends set off on their road trip. They started from Chicago and drove to Nashville, where they spent the night at a hotel 8. When they arrived at the hotel Chuck got everyone checked in and situated and then they went for dinner. Since it was the first time any of them had been to Nashville, they decided to first check out a few of the local landmarks. They made a detour to Memphis to see the home of Elvis Presley, the King of Rock and Roll; it was one of the biggest houses they had ever seen. The next stop, which was Chuck's idea, was the Grand Ole Opry. Being a huge fan of country music, Chuck enjoyed this visit more than the rest. After sight seeing they went to the Lodgers Steakhouse for dinner. They all had steaks and drinks, the great food was accompanied by old stories and the good times they had had during college. It was now going on midnight, they all decided to head back to the hotel. Steven, Harper and Gloria all went up to their rooms to get some rest, Chuck and Christy stayed up for a bit longer. "I'm really looking forward to getting to that island. I like the name of it, it sounds kinda freaky doesn't it?" Chuck said to a very tired Christy.

"It does a little bit. For some reason I get goosebumps when I think about it. How did you find this place? I know you said you found it on the Internet but what were you searching for?" Christy yawned as she finished her sentence.

"Actually, I got bored while I was island hunting and started looking up random stuff and got a strange text from an unknown number. I checked out the text and it led me to the website for the island. I think I was looking stuff up about vampires or something supernatural." Chuck himself chuckled at what he said. " Don't worry it's not like the island is haunted or infested with rabid bats that are waiting to suck your blood. It had some old urban legend from way back in the day. But come on, we both know all that scary shit doesn't really exist. I promise nothing is going to happen." Even though he said nothing would happen, Chuck still had a lingering feeling that wouldn't go away.

"I know it doesn't exist, smartass." Christy declared before she threw a pillow at Chuck.

They used the pillows to fight each other and lighten the mood after a very short but unsettling conversation. They went back and forth, shot for shot but Christy gave up first. As she was about to surrender Chuck got one last blow that seemingly knocked her on to the bed in defeat. Chuck, also out of breath, fell down next to her on one of the queen sized beds. For a few moments they just laid there, silence engulfed the room. Chuck looked over at Christy, who was already looking back at him. "There is something I have been wanting to do for years," Chuck said as he moved closer and gently held her face and passionately kissed her. After the kiss they both, mostly surprised, just stared into each other's eyes smiling. As Christy moved in to return the kiss there was a pounding on the door that made the both of them jump. They both shot their heads towards the door, but Chuck didn't react as fast as Christy did and he saw a look of fear and surprise in her face.

"Who's there?" Chuck asked in a demanding voice. He was hoping his tone would make Christy feel safer with him there.

"It's me, Steven. I think you have my suitcase because I don't own any hillbilly music."

At the same time, they both started laughing, only Christy's laugh was more relief than humor. Chuck got up and opened the door to let Steven into the room.

"How the hell did you get our bags mixed up? Mine is black and you have a blue one, plus mine has a travel tag with my name on it. We may be related but we don't have the same name."

"Yeah yeah yeah I know. It's because I was in a hurry to get out of the car cuz I had to take a leak. I grabbed the only other bag that looked like mine. Don't worry Chuckie, I didn't go through anything. I saw some CDs that weren't mine and knew it was your bag. Besides you're the only hillbilly here with your yeehaw country music." Steve was trying to make fun of his cousin in front of his crush. Steven knew that Chuck had a huge crush on Christy and he was picking on him for it.

"First of all, don't call me Chuckie, I'm not 5. And it's not hillbilly music, it's country music. You weren't the only one wanting out of the car and next time you come banging on the door like the cops, you're gonna be gettin a whoopin cuz." By this time Chuck was putting on a show for Christy. He had seen how scared she had gotten when Steven banged on the door and he was trying to comfort her. "Now take your bag and get. I need some sleep and we have a long trip ahead of us." Chuck booted his cousin out the door in a joking way.

Now in their own beds, Chuck and Christy finally went to sleep. Both were out almost immediately.

That night Chuck dreamt about the island. He dreamt that there was someone or something that called him there. There was a woman with long flowing blonde hair, skin that almost seemed pale in the moonlight, which was as smooth as a petal from a rose. Her hazel blue eyes, which stood out the most, were so mesmerizing that even in a dream they seemed to hypnotize him. Her stare felt so real and so close that Chuck awoke paranoid fully expecting to see a woman standing over his bed. Oddly enough that wasn't far from the truth, when he opened his eyes he did see a woman. That woman was Christy, she said that he was making weird noises in his sleep that woke her up.

"Sorry I woke you, I was having a very weird dream but I think it's over now." As he apologized he noticed a look of concern on Christy's face. Like any good gentleman, he asked her if she was ok? She said she was but he could tell she was still worried. "Do you want to sleep next to me tonight?" Chuck asked shyly. "I'm asking because you seem worried about something. So, if you want you can bunk with me, but only if you want to." Chuck smiled because he could see that she was already moving the sheets to lay down next to him. She laid her head on his chest, placed her hand on his left shoulder and he wrapped his arm around her. And for the first time in their friendship, they fell asleep in each other's arms.

In the morning Christy woke up to the sound of the shower running and Chuck singing a country song. She laid in bed listening to Chuck sing, she could tell immediately that it was a country love song. She felt like he was singing to her or at least she hoped he was. After a few more lines she finally figured out what song he was singing. It was also one of her favorite songs so she quietly, in her softest voice, began singing with him.

While in the shower, he heard a noise, the sweet sound of Christy singing. He had never heard her sing outside of times at school. As soothing as her beautiful voice was, what he didn't realize was that she was practically whispering the words to the song and he shouldn't have been able to hear her. Not knowing this he wrapped his towel around himself and came out of the bathroom applauding her singing and startled her.

"How did you know I was singing? I wasn't even singing loud, if anything I was whispering." Her face was apple red and she was extremely freaked out by the fact that Chuck could hear her singing.

"What do you mean you were whispering? I could hear you loud and clear from the bathroom and I had the door closed. There is no way that you were whispering, unless I have superpowers and I can hear through walls."

"Well, I don't know how you heard me but I was whispering and you definitely don't have superpowers."

"OK. Well, let's get ready. After I get some clothes on, I'm going to make sure everyone is up and moving so we can hit the road. Right now, it's 7am. I figure if we're on the road by 8am we can make it to Orlando by 5 or 6 tonight." Chuck was now talking to Christy from the bathroom where he was getting dressed. "Hey, I'm gonna hit the breakfast area on the way back up. Do you want anything?"

"Coffee would be amazing! And maybe a bagel, if they have any. Please and thank you." Christy was still trying to figure out how Chuck had heard her. As Chuck left the room, she made her way to the bathroom to take a quick shower and get ready to get their road trip on its way.

"There was no way he could have been able to hear me, I wasn't even singing that loud." Christy couldn't shake the notion that he had heard her singing. "Maybe the walls are super thin. Oh well." She dismissed the thought and finished her shower. As she got out of the shower she called Chuck's name to see if he was in the room. With no answer she exited the bathroom to get dressed. On the bed she found a single white rose laying next to her bagel. "Aww how sweet!" She said as she picked up the rose and inhaled its sweet aroma. She finished getting dressed and loaded her stuff up in the car.

Chuck headed back to the room to check on Christy and see if they forgot anything. When he got to the room he was surprised to see her sitting on his bed waiting for him. "Everything ok? Did you get the little present I left you? Last night was the first time we've ever slept together, even though we didn't do anything, and it was the first time we've ever kissed. Call me mushy but it was kinda special or romantic. And that kiss was amazing." Chuck nervously smiled at Christy.

She got up from the bed, slowly walked towards Chuck, smiled at him and softly kissed him. "That was for the rose and last night was special to me too. I'm glad we didn't do anything." With a mischievous grin Christy added one last word that left Chuck speechless. "Yet." She then walked out of the room to go check on Gloria and Harper.

Chuck just stood there, speechless and smiling, and his imagination raced trying to figure out what that "yet" could mean. Nevertheless, he was just happy that she liked the rose and really happy that she had kissed him. He started getting his bags, when all of a sudden he felt the presence of someone in the room with him. He smiled thinking it was Christy but as he glanced over his right shoulder he saw a woman standing in front of the window. Normally that wouldn't bother him but in an instant she was now standing inside the room. "Can I help you?" Chuck asked the oddly quiet woman. As he looked at her, Chuck had this strange feeling of deja vu that he had either seen or met her before. The woman was at least 5' 9", she had long wavy blonde hair, hazel blue eyes. There was something about her eyes that seemed to be calling out to him. She took a few steps towards him and when she stopped her hair was moving as if being blown by the wind. Chuck could feel his heart pounding his chest as she stood there. He took a step forward and the beautiful woman vanished, like she had never been there at all.

Christy was already on her way back to the room, from talking to Gloria and Harper. She was so happy that things were starting to look good for her and Chuck. She had waited for this to happen for so long, since the day they had met she had a crush on him and lately it felt like a lot more than a crush. When she got back to the room, Chuck was in the bathroom splashing water on his face. His face was pale, almost ghostlike, as if he had seen something that scared him. She ran over to him and was asking if he was ok, what happened, what's the matter and all kinds of worried questions.

"I'm fine, I just saw something that freaked me out. It's gone now, so I'm ok."

"What did you see? What freaked you out?"

With some hesitation in his voice, Chuck told Christy what happened. "I was getting my stuff together so I could put it in the car and some chick came into the room. She just stood there, then she took a few steps towards me and then she vanished."

"What do you mean she vanished?"

"I mean she was in the room one minute and the next she was gone. She disappeared, like she was never there. I know she was there because I saw her with my own two eyes and I am not going crazy. I know I've done and said some pretty weird things before but I swear to you I really seen this lady... this ghost or whatever she was, disappear." At this point Chuck's face was red from ranting about his vanishing visitor. As he stood there he noticed the look on Christy's face, she looked worried, scared and as if she was trying to make sense of what she had just heard. He felt bad about the worried look on her face. He did the only thing he could think of, he held her. He held her tight and close, even though it was his fault for her reaction and scaring her, all he could think of was comforting her.

"How could he have seen a ghost, they don't even exist." Her mind was racing with what she had just heard. "As long as he's ok, that's all that matters." Christy couldn't tell if Chuck was serious at first but the look on his face proved that he was. "Are you sure you're ok? I mean, are you going to be able to drive or should I drive?" Trying not to show how worried she was. Christy decided to play off Chuck's brief moment of insanity. "Unless you want to let Steven, Gloria or Harper drive while we sit in the back and let you relax?" Christy said this with other intentions in mind. They had yet to talk about last night and she wanted to see what he was thinking about them.

Chuck wasn't one to turn down the assistance of a beautiful lady plus he was still a bit shaken from the events that had just unfolded. "We can do that, you know if they don't mind driving while we relax." Chuck somehow knew that she had already gotten the ok from the others. Chuck put his stuff into the trunk of the suv and slid into the backseat with Christy. The five friends continued on their road trip, hoping to reach their next destination by 5 or 6pm. They made a quick stop at wal-mart to grab some drinks and snacks. Christy bought a pillow so that Chuck could relax while they talked.

Now that they were back in the vehicle they were off.

"How are you feeling?" Christy asked

"Much better. Thank you. I'm sorry about that whole situation. I'm not sure what had happened. It was like a dream but so very real and scary." Chuck started apologizing about the whole ghost thing. "But let's not talk about that. I'd like to talk about that kiss. It was absolutely amazing." Chuck was smiling from ear to ear as he said that and he could see that Christy was to. " I'm not gonna lie, I have been wanting to do that for years."

"Well, since we're being honest, so have I. Lately I have felt like something between us has been growing. And last night laying next to you, it just felt so right." Christy was scared to tell Chuck that, not knowing what he was going to say.

"You took the words right out of my mouth. Just holding you and the feel of your head laying on my chest, there are no words to describe how amazing it felt. Maybe if you would like to, when we get to the island we could have or I mean go on a date. I know it's a vacation but we could turn this into something more." Now it was Chuck's turn to be nervous and a little bit scared.

"I would really like that. I have been waiting for you to ask me out for like forever." Christy let out a nervous giggle. Chuck sat up, leaned towards Christy and gently kissed her.

"Get a room you two." Steven yelled back to them. "It's about damn time. We've known this moment was bound to happen but damn what took so long."

"Shut up. Let them have their moment, it's beautiful." Harper yelled at Steven for being a smartass.

"Thanks guys." Christy thanked their friends for the support. But like they had said it had taken a while for them to see what everyone else had for a while.

About an hour later both Chuck and Christy had fallen asleep, again in each other's arms. Everything was going fine, Steven and Gloria switched places as driver. Suddenly Chuck started making an odd moaning noise, they thought he was trying to be funny since he and Christy were all the way in the back of the suv they rented. But unfortunately, the disappearing lady, as Chuck called her, was back. But this time something was very different.

It was a bright night, thanks to the glow of a full moon. Chuck was walking on the beach, the mist of the waves slapping the shore filled the air. Chuck soon realized he wasn't alone, someone was walking next to him. He was hoping that when he looked over he would see Christy next to him but he wasn't so lucky. Next to him, matching him step for step was the tall blonde from the hotel room. As much as he wanted to turn and run from this ghostly woman, he didn't. They both stopped waking in sync. Chuck was scared yet oddly calm. When he looked into the woman's eyes he saw something very familiar in them. It was like they had known each other before but he couldn't figure out from where. There was a longing for her that he did not understand and a burning hatred that rivaled the intense feelings of attraction. He took a single step backwards and that's when she spoke to him.

"Hello Charles. It has been a long time, hasn't it? You do not remember me do you? That is all right because very soon my love, you shall. I promise you."

"How do you know my name? Why do I feel like I know you? Who are you? What's your name?" Chuck shakily asked the mystery woman.

"Because you do know me, my sweet. You and I have quite the history"

" But how? From where? Please answer me."

"Alright, but first you must calm yourself. What is my name? My name is...."

"Chuck, wake up! Wake up, you're scaring me. Please wake up." Christy had been yelling so loud that she hadn't even noticed that the car was now parked on the shoulder of the expressway. Now screaming at the top of her lungs, Chuck's eyes started to slowly blink open.

"What's going on? Where am I? Where did she go?" Feeling very disoriented, Chuck was trying to get a grip on reality. Although he didn't remember falling asleep, he had been out for over 2 hours. He still wasn't sure what was real at the moment because his dream was so vivid and felt so real.

"Why didn't you wake up? What the hell, you scared the crap out of me. First we fell asleep and I woke up cuz you were twitching like you were having a seizure or something. And who were you talking to or about? You kept mumbling and I couldn't make out what you were saying." Christy was so scared, paranoid and worried that she said everything in one quick breath. As afraid as she was for Chuck, part of her was jealous that he was dreaming about a woman other than her. But jealousy was going to have to wait, what Chuck was about to say would make her question his sanity.

"Take it easy Christy, I'm still trying to figure out what's going on. I barely remember what happened. First, like you said, we fell asleep but all of a sudden I was in complete darkness. I thought one of you guys were playing a trick on me and put something over my face. But when I went to move whatever was covering my face I realized that there wasn't anything there. Just darkness. Then, I blinked and I was on a beach walking. I looked around for anyone but the only person I saw was the ghost lady from the hotel. She was walking right next to me, matching me step for step. We stopped walking and she spoke. She knew my name and she knew me somehow. I started asking her questions and she was about to answer me and then I heard you calling my name." Chuck looked at Christy. "The sound of your voice is what woke me up. When I finally came to, I had no idea what was going on. I could barely tell what was real. It was like I had amnesia or something. I didn't mean to scare anyone and I am really sorry. But that dream or whatever it was, was so intense and vivid." Chuck looked into Christy's eyes as he apologized to everyone. The whole time Chuck was telling them about his dream, he was still trying to figure out who this mysterious woman was. Obviously she knew him, but he felt like he had known her for a lifetime.

Christy couldn't help but feel bad for yelling at Chuck, but she was scared and she panicked. She even scared everyone else in the vehicle. She apologized to Chuck for yelling at him and she apologized to everyone else for scaring them half to death.

They pulled off of the shoulder and continued driving. They made a quick stop at a gas station. Christy and Chuck remained in the backseat of the suv, talking about his dream and trying to make sense of it. Both agreed to not fall asleep til they go to their destination. Harper took a turn driving while Gloria and Steven were acting as copilots. An ominous feeling lingered in the air as they drove on. The woman was still haunting his mind and no matter how much he tried to focus on Christy, she was still there in the shadows of his mind.

Chapter Two

It had been hours since Chuck dreamt about his mystery woman and he was grateful for that. He was thinking about how he and Christy had gotten closer than he would have imagined. At one point they had both fallen asleep, but this time something had kept him from dreaming about his mystery woman. He figured it had something to do with him and Christy sleeping on each other, as if she was a dreamcatcher filtering out this woman. He thought their arms made the circle of the dreamcatcher, their fingers interlocked made the knots keeping it together and at the center were their hearts keeping him strong. It made him feel good about not dreaming of someone other than Christy. Even though he still wondered who the strange woman was, he tried not to dwell on it so he wouldn't miss this moment with her.

It was already noon and Steven had pulled into a rest area so they could stretch their legs and have some lunch. Chuck had packed a cooler with lunch meat, pop and some apples and oranges. He had also brought a few of the party size bags of Doritos, some bread and other ingredients for their sandwiches. They each ate two sandwiches and all of the chips that Chuck had bought as well as a twelve pack of pop. After they ate, Chuck and Christy walked around the rest area talking about how they felt about each other and how long they felt this way.

"I've had feelings for you since we first met. It started out as a little crush, but it grew into so much more. I can't stand being away from you and when we are together I feel like I'm the only person in the world. The way you make me smile, laugh, how you make me feel like I am actually seen and heard. I think I am in love with you. Actually, I know I love you."

Christy could barely believe what Chuck had just told her. He bared his heart and soul to her and everything he told her was exactly how she felt about him.

"This is probably going to sound crazy but everything you just told to me is exactly how I feel about you. You mean the world to me and I love you too." Christy's heart was pounding so fast. As scared as she felt she was able to get the nerve to move closer to chuck and gently kissed him on the lips. It was the perfect moment until Chuck said one name.

When Christy kissed Chuck he was overwhelmed and somewhere in the rush of emotions, his mystery woman came to him and whispered her name to him. Right at the same time Christy had kissed him and when she moved back the only thing he said was "Cassandra" and he hit the floor.

"Chuck, wake up, snap out of it! Guys, get over here quick!" Christy, frantically screaming, was trying to help Chuck while trying not to punch him for saying someone else's name.

"What happened? What's wrong with Chuck?" Steven was drilling Christy and he was worried about his cousin. Harper and Gloria stood back almost in tears because Chuck looked pale as a ghost.

"We were talking and I kissed him. When I moved back; he said the name Cassandra and passed out. I've tried shaking him, yelling at him, I even accidentally smacked him, nothing has worked. The only idea I have left is to throw some water on him, but I don't have any." When Christy looked up, she saw that Gloria had a water bottle in her hands. She was about to take the bottle and fill it with water from the cooler but instead she just grabbed the whole cooler and dumped it on Chuck.

Chuck sat up gasping for air. The icy water had snapped him out of whatever episode he was having and shocked his system back to normal. "Holy shit. That was freezing cold. Who dumped that on me." Chuck was already shivering from the ice cold bath he just took.

"Sorry, that was me, but you deserved it you asshole. Why did you say "Cassandra" after I kissed you? Why did you pass out? What is wrong with you?" Christy was getting mad at Chuck for something he had no control over.

"I honestly don't know why I passed out. I think I had some kind of emotional overload or something. Everything you told me was flooding my head. Then when you kissed me, I saw you and then you turned into this ghost girl from the hotel and said "My name is Cassandra!" Then I had a flash of memories but they were from the 1800s and then they jumped to the past few days. The next thing I know I'm getting some cold ass water thrown on me. So, what's wrong with me? I think I'm being haunted by some chick I knew, somehow, from the 1800s. I think I'm going crazy."

"Well crazy or not we need to get going or we're not going to make our flight. And if we're not going to make the flight we need to call the airport so we can change our flight plans. So, everybody off your asses and into the car. Harper, you're driving because I'm tired of driving." Steven took control of the situation and was trying to get everybody's attention off of his crazy cousin.

Before they got to the car Chuck thanked his cousin and tried talking to Christy but she was either still mad at him or she was trying to figure out if he was making up his story or not.

"Christy, I know you probably don't believe my story but you have to try to. I would never lie to you or ever do anything to hurt you. You have to know that. You mean more to me than anything in this world and I don't know why this is happening to me. What I do know is that it is happening and I need you with me, that is the only way I can make it through. Please believe me." Chuck was pleading to Christy with all his heart.

"I'm trying, but how can you have memories from the 1800's? That plus some ghost bimbo haunting your dreams and freaking you out. It's like something out of a movie or a book. It is just weird, but no matter how weird it is," she paused for a moment to look Chuck in the eyes, "I am here for you."

With a breath of relief, Chuck thanks Christy. "You have no idea how relieved and happy I am that you said that. Thank you so very much. So, where should we start?

"I'd say with the memories. What happened in them and what does she want with you?" Christy was doing her best to be logical about what was going on but it all seemed so strange. Part of her doubted him but another part wanted so badly to believe what he was saying.

So, they began trying to solve the mystery of the haunted dreams and forgotten memories. They unknowingly set themselves down a path that would test the true strengths of friendship and love. Unfortunately, theirs would be tested and pushed to and past those limits.

Chuck had begun telling her about a man, whom he assumed was meant to be him or had once been, and his search for love and family. He told her about his journey through neighboring towns and the massacre he had seen in the town of Wills where fifty-six people were brutally murdered in a church and saloon. Then he started telling Christy how this man met Cassandra and that they eventually were married and had a daughter. He couldn't remember the daughters name but he did know that she had passed away at a young age. "After the daughter passed everything starts to blur and I can't remember anything else. I feel like she won't let me remember anything else and she is hiding something. She's definitely keeping me from remembering anything else about her, as if she only wanted me to remember the good stuff." He sat there more confused now than before he started talking about the supposed memories. "There is one more thing, it has something to do with her eyes. Every time she appears, it's her eyes that seem to hypnotize me or put me in some kind of a trance. After that, I can't help but go to her. I'm sorry." Chuck looked down with shame and a hint of defeat in his eyes. It honestly scares me, to think that one of these times when I go to sleep or slip off in a daydream, somehow I won't be able to come back."

The thought of dying or not coming back from a dream literally scared him. One reason was that he actually loved Christy and he didn't know why but he sensed he had some feelings for Cassandra as well. He was confused, how can you love someone so much and still have feelings for someone else who may not even be real. He also realized that all this had started happening at the time when he and Christy started getting closer. The day in the hotel when they first kissed was the first time he saw Cassandra. Could it be possible that a love from a past life had come back through his dreams because of Christy? Did Cassandra decide to come back out of jealousy or was it something more?

While Chuck was thinking about his Christy and Cassandra theory, Steven had called the airport and rescheduled their flights. Harper had pulled onto the shoulder of the expressway and Steven had taken over driving duties. They weren't quite ready to let Chuck get back behind the wheel even with the daylight they had left, they were unsure. Harper quickly fell asleep next to her sister once Steven started driving. Despite her best efforts to stay awake, Christy fell asleep while she was leaning against Chuck. Chuck had opened a pop that he had bought from the rest stop earlier and was hoping that the caffeine would keep him awake and away from his chaotic dreamland.

Unfortunately, he now found himself standing on a white sandy beach right after sunset. He cursed himself for falling asleep, the scene of the moon rising and the waves hitting the shore was truly magnificent but what was lurking and out of sight was what he feared the most. He began walking down the beach. He figured all he could do now was search for answers and hope with all his might that he wakes up from this dreamscape.

As he walked the shoreline, watching the waves roll in and back out, he noticed someone in the water. He wasn't close enough to see a face but deep down he already knew who it was. He walked closer, his heart started beating faster and breathing had increased, he started to feel dizzy. He fell forward landing on his knees and felt the air filling his lungs thicken making it harder to breathe. He tried to calm himself but failed as he saw the figure moving towards him.

"Are you ok?"

"I….I…. can't…..breathe!" That was all Chuck could get himself to say as he gasped for breath between each word.

"Ok, lie down on your back and just focus on the stars. They will calm your nerves and steady your breathing."

As he looked up at the star filled sky, the clouds seemed to part just for him giving him the most spectacular view. He began to feel his heart slow down and the air was slowly thinning.

“You remember me now, don’t you? I'm guessing you can only recall bits and pieces, fragments of time but not everything. That is because I am only allowing your mind to see what I choose to show you.” Cassandra made it perfectly clear that even in his dreams she had control of his mind.

“Why?” Chuck was now able to breathe better. “What are you trying to hide from me Cassandra? I know it has something to do with your eyes, you somehow hypnotize me and are able to draw me to you. I know that is part of your secret or whatever it that you are hiding. Right?”

“It appears you and your, is it, Christy have been working harder than I thought. Unless, you figured that out on your own. But that would mean you’re not being completely honest with her. Hmm… I think you might just realize more than you're letting on and not telling her to either keep her safe or yourself. You didn’t want to frighten her. You’ve always been sensitive to the ones you love Charles. It was one of the qualities that made me love you so much. Although, you have a darker side that you may not yet be familiar with. A side so dark that you sent a loved one so far away and left them to suffer in solitude.

Something you once did to me many many years ago. But I do not seek vengeance my dear, I only seek to find something I once lost." Cassandra finished her plea with her back to him. She did this because she didn't want him to see her in her true form and she was not being truthful with him. She knew that her Charles was in there, he knew when she wasn't being honest and was not sure if Chuck was able to see the same or not.

"If not for revenge, then why have you come back? And don't give me some lost love story, I want the truth. I CAN tell when you're lying, you were never good at it anyways. I can remember that much. I want you to remember something, you are in my dreams and I control my dreams. Why don't you just tell me the truth? About yourself, about me or maybe I should ask you about Chloe or about Wills. If I remember correctly, there was only one direct route from Syrus to Brooks and it was straight through Wills. Am I getting closer, my dear wife." Chuck was starting to get mad and with that anger he remembered that they were once married.

"You remember much more than I thought you would dearest. Yes, there was only one route to Wills. Yes, the massacre you remember seeing was done by myself.

Those men in that saloon tried to force themselves on me. And as you saw, I was not without my own protection, I killed every last one of them. My only regret was killing your driver, Edward. He rushed behind me as I was feeding and I thought he was another one of the townspeople trying to attack me. I responded quickly and without thought and killed him." Cassandra had a wild and animalistic look in her eyes, as if the thought of her kills excited her.

Chuck had not yet regained that memory. As the words came out of her mouth, it came charging back to his mind making his knees buckle as he hit the sand. With a storm of emotions, anger, sadness, disbelief and even hate, he glared at her. Chuck lunged at her but came nowhere close to touching her. Unlike everything else in his dream, Cassandra's presence, whether she was dead or alive, was merely spectral. He flew right through her and landed face first in the sand. "You know how you can tell when you truly HATE someone?" Chuck now looking directly into her eyes, "it's when you've loved them with all your heart and so deeply but all that good has vanished. I hate you Cassandra. I wish I had never met you."

She swallowed his words like swallowing a stone that sat heavily in your stomach. Filled with anger, her eyes went from hazel blue to the brightest blue he had ever seen. Two of her teeth on the top row began to extend slowly. She began to inch closer to him, the rage in her eyes burned like fire. “You think you are in control just because we are in your head. Dear husband, you have no idea what I am capable of. In your head or in person I am the one with the power. Not you!” She pounced at him with immense speed, since he was still on the ground he was an easy target. Much to his terror, she was able to knock him on his back. She gripped his throat tightly with one hand, pinning him to the ground. With her free hand she grabbed his face and turned his head to the side. She was about to sink her teeth into his neck when he vanished from her grip. “For now, Charles, but very soon you shall belong to me.”

“CHRISTY!!! Oh my god. I’m awake. Thank you Jesus.” The one thing that he could think of was what saved him from that insane nightmare. Now wide awake with tears rolling down his face. Christy stared at him, wide eyed with her mouth slightly open, as if she had seen Cassandra herself or a ghost.

“Ummm. Chuck. I’m so sorry that I didn’t believe you. I don’t even know where to start but no matter what we will beat this. We will beat it together.” Christy was filled with fear, disbelief, and adrenaline. She was awakened by Chuck struggling in his sleep. Marks began to appear on his neck as if he was being choked but no one in the car was choking him. They just appeared out of nowhere.

"What the fuck, she is absolutely insane. She tried to kill me or turn me into a vampire or whatever she is. She had her hand on my throat and was pinning me down on the sand with one damn hand." Chuck was frantically yelling about his nightmare. He was so loud that he woke up Harper and Gloria. Steven panicked and made the car swerve before he was able to pull over in a gas station parking lot. "Well at least now I know why I am obsessed with vampires, I was married to one. But why come back now, it doesn't make sense, nothing has happened lately that would concern my dead vampire wife. Except…." Just then he looked directly at Christy. "Except us. Us getting closer and the kiss. Maybe us getting closer is a threat to her somehow. When she was attacking me, the first thing I thought of was you and then I woke up."

Chuck was beginning to think that Christy was a threat to Cassandra and whatever plans she had for him. Was Christy in danger? Chuck was more than just worried, he was terrified. He was especially worried about his past, Cassandra said something about him sending her far away. She was clearly furious about the situation and she seemed set on having her revenge. But how was she planning on getting her revenge? Could she kill him in his dreams, before today he didn't even think vampires were real, so the idea of being murdered in his dreams was quite horrifying. Even the thought of her biting him and turning him into a vampire sent chills down his spine. His imagination was in overdrive and it was freaking him out. There were so many ways she could get him but only in his dreams. Unless she found a way to resurrect herself or if she never actually died. Thankfully she could only haunt him in his dreams, for now.

"Hey, are you ok? You're awfully quiet and it's kinda freaking me out. Anything you want to talk about?" Christy was nervous, scared and worried for Chuck. She had never seen him like this, he seemed so lost. "Don't forget, I am here for you and you're not alone."

He smiled at her, "Thank you. I truly appreciate you more than you know." With Christy trying to grasp the reality of what has happened, he started to feel a little bit relieved. Though with her at his side, would it put her in

Cassandra's path for revenge? He wasn't sure if he should be alone to deal with this or let Christy be there with him for whatever came next. "You know, if this becomes too much for you, I wouldn't be mad if you did whatever you had to do to keep yourself safe. Honestly, I would never forgive myself if you got hurt because of me."

"I said I was here for you and that's where I plan to stay. You and I, we got this." Christy smirked, "Whatever this may be, we face it together. Got it?

"Yes ma'am, I got it."

At that moment Chuck looked out the window and let out a heavy sigh. While he was busy racking his brain over the current situation he didn't realize how far they had driven. His stomach dropped as he read the sign passing them. "Leaving Nashville, Entering Logan, TN". At first he began to wonder why he was having this feeling, a feeling of familiarity, comfort and dread. In a literal blink of an eye, it hit him like a freight train. A memory that followed the feeling in the pit of his stomach. He knew this town. Much to his surprise, as well as everyone else in the car, he said out loud what he was thinking.

"I'm home!"

Chapter Three

Since Steven had called the airport to reschedule their flight at the rest stop. They still had another day to get there but the flight was later in the evening. The airport gave him hell about switching flights, but Steven was able to get them to switch the departure time.

Chuck was grateful and scared. Grateful because he would have a little extra time to spend with Christy but scared because it meant Cassandra had that much more time for whatever she was planning. And it took an awful lot to scare him. What scared him even more was the route Harper had taken. The moment they left Nashville and entered Logan, he knew that things were going to get worse.

Just then Christy woke up, looked around and asked. "Where are we?”

Chuck answered “Home!”

“What? What do you mean home? I thought you were born in Chicago.” Christy was confused and could tell what Chuck was thinking because he had a blank stare as he looked out the window.

"Yeah I was born in Chicago but way before then I lived here. I lived here in a big house with Cassandra. It's where she told me her secret, where our daughter was born and where she died." Chuck had started crying when he mentioned his long passed daughter. "She was so young. The doctors couldn't figure out what was wrong with her. We brought in so many doctors to try and figure out what was wrong. Cassandra blamed herself for Chloe's death. But I, Charles, never did. He loved them both with all of his heart." Drying off his tears Chuck looked at Christy and she too was crying. "Sorry, that was a bit much to unload but so many memories are just flooding my brain. I don't know how to deal with it all."

"Harper, can you stop the car please?" He waited for a response but clearly she was ignoring his request. "Stop the damn car.... please." Chuck's sudden request had everyone puzzled.

"Why? What for?" Asked Harper in a demanding yet somewhat concerned tone

"What's going on?" Steven asked in a sleepy voice

"Chuck sweetie, what's wrong? Why do you wanna stop the car?" Christy asked, still wiping away a few remaining tears.

"Just stop the car, I'm fine, I just need some air." Chuck was getting a little aggravated by all the questions.

Then Gloria set him off.

"Open a damn window, we don't have time for you to take a stroll down memory lane. DAMN I knew I should have stayed home."

"STOP THE FUCKING CAR!!" Chuck had had enough. "I rented the damn car, so pull this piece of shit over right fuckin now."

Harper pulled over as fast as she could and Chuck stormed out of the car.

"What the hell is his problem? Am I the only one who thinks he is making all this crap up? I mean come on Vampires, past lives and some chick haunting his dreams. Someone has seen too many scary movies, he needs some serious therapy." Gloria ranted about Chuck and everything that he claimed is happening to him.

"Gloria, what is your problem? He isn't making any of this up." Christy had come to Chuck's defense. "I saw marks appear on him from out of nowhere. You don't see the fear in his eyes every time he wakes up and has dreamt about her. He is not crazy, he's not lying, and I love him. So, if you have a problem either keep it to yourself or go home. We can easily drop you off at a bus or train station. Shit, you can walk if you're going to keep being a bitch."

After about 20 minutes Chuck returned to the car. "I'm sorry you guys. I shouldn't have gone off like that. I am really sorry."

"It's ok"

"No, it's not Christy," Gloria yelled. "He's freakin me out and I don't know about the rest of you but I'm about ready to go home. This is Insane."

"Gloria…"

"No Christy, She's right." Chuck stopped Christy before she could defend him. "This IS insane. It's just some bad dreams. I'll try to keep them under control. I'm sorry. There's a rest stop up ahead, how 'bout I treat you guys to some junk food." Chuck was trying to lighten the mood and he did.

“Sounds good to me.” Steven and Harper said at the same time, breaking the silence.

They did stop at the rest stop. They got pops, candy, and chips. Chuck told them to wait in the car while he paid. After they left he asked the attendant for a bottle of “stay awake” pills. He figured if he didn’t sleep, he wouldn’t dream and freak out his friends. He especially didn’t wanna freak out Christy.

So, after paying, he popped a couple pills and returned to the car with the snacks. And their journey continued.

From that point on, everything was going smoother. They were going through Logan with no problem and planned to spend the night in Xavier. As they drove, Gloria pointed out a big mansion that was looming in the distance. Chuck didn’t even mention that the big mansion they were all gawking at used to be his house.

He stared intensely at it as they passed, slowing down to truly admire its beauty and imagining the history. He closed his eyes while looking at it and saw Cassandra, he remembered their room, Chloe's room and the servants quarters behind the house. As they drove by he saw someone standing in the window and to him, it looked like Cassandra. He quickly took two more pills and chugged the rest of his pop.

They decided to get something to eat at a local restaurant that had been around since the 1850s. It had been remodeled several times over the years but it remained in the same family of owners. While they waited for a table, Chuck and Christy began looking at pictures ranging from 1850 to the present. They started with the present pictures. A few famous people, newlyweds and families. Further down the wall were older pictures. When Chuck and Christy reached the end of the wall they found a picture of a young man and a young woman. The names read "Charles and Cassandra Jones".

"OH MY GOD!" Christy was in shock. "He looks exactly like you. It's like… like…"

"Looking into a mirror. That's her. That's Cassandra, the woman from my dreams." Oddly enough Chuck was calm. He knew he had been to that restaurant before but forgot he had been there with Cassandra. It was right after they got married, sort of their honeymoon. "Umm… Let's not mention this to the others."

“Yeah, that's a good idea. They would probably pack up and leave.”

“Our table is ready.” Steven startled both Chuck and Christy. “Damn you two lovebirds are jumpy. C’mon I’m hungry.”

During dinner the picture was never brought up. The five friends talked about crazy parties, crazy parents, one night stands, crazy exes, and all kinds of nights that they dared to share. At the moment Steven was in the lead for the craziest night.

He had gone to a rock concert a few years ago. While he was there he hooked up with some chick and her friend. After the concert they went to a bar and got way too drunk. After that he could only recall bits and pieces of the night. He remembered going back to the other girl's apartment. All three of them get into the shower, and lots of moaning and sex. But when they woke up, the girls didn’t remember him and they kicked him out of the apartment half naked.

Everyone had a good laugh at his crazy night. At one point Chuck started yawning, so he excused himself from the table and went to the restroom. When he got there, he went to the sink and splashed some water on his face. He was about to take a couple more stay awake pills, when he looked up from the sink in the mirror there she stood, Cassandra. Looking directly at Chuck from the mirror where his reflection should have been. He shot around expecting to see her standing behind him but no one was there. He slowly turned back to the mirror.

"Ahh… What the fuck. How are you doing that? Why can't you just leave me alone? What do you want?" Chuck stammered backwards yelling at the ghostly reflection.

"My dear Charles, you have come home. In this place we ate as a happily married couple, full of love and a bright future together. You drove past our home, where our daughter was born and where she died. Our beautiful Chloe." Cassandra began to cry, even as a ghost in the mirror her tears seemed to roll off of her face and down the mirror, her tears pooled onto the counter. "Do you remember our Chloe, my love?"

"Yes… I do remember her." Chuck got watery eyed. "And I remember what you told me after she died. Your dark secret." Chuck felt the sadness in his heart being replaced by anger. "And I remember what you did to Jacob.

You… you monster. He was an innocent boy and you murdered him." Chuck rushed forward and punched the mirror, shattering it and cutting his hand, he bled out on the floor.

Realizing what he had done, he wrapped his hand with paper towels and rushed out of the bathroom. Luckily, no one had heard him yelling in the bathroom or the sound of the mirror breaking. He lied to the manager and said he slipped in the bathroom and caught himself on the counter and mirror. The manager apologized repeatedly and offered to give them their meal for free. Chuck refused the offer stating it was an accident and he didn't want anything for free.

When he got back to the table, he tried to hide his hand, but everyone had noticed the blood soaked paper towels. The restaurant manager even came over to apologize again. He said it was unacceptable that he slipped on some water and he comped the meal regardless of what Chuck said. The manager said he was going to inform the waiter and whatever they wanted was on the house. The manager told him not to worry about the mirror but did bring up something Chuck had hoped he wouldn't.

"Sir, I couldn't help but notice you bear a striking resemblance to a former customer of ours. When my relatives first opened this establishment two of our frequent guests were a newlywed couple. I believe their names were Charles and his wife Cassandra"

"Really, are you shitting me?" Gloria shouted out "Seriously are you sure?"

"I am most definitely sure ma'am. It is truly uncanny how much the gentlemen resemble one another. There is a picture of the couple on our wall. If you would like to see for yourselves."

Chuck and Christy just looked at each other in disbelief. They both had hoped the picture wouldn't be brought up. They had hoped they would make it out of the restaurant without the others seeing it. But unfortunately, luck was not on their side.

"Hell yeah we wanna see it." demanded Gloria. She was hoping that the picture would force Chuck to talk about what was going on and why he had been freaking out ever since they started this vacation. "Maybe we can finally get someone to start talking about what's really going on. Or maybe this is all one big practical joke. I mean this whole trip was planned by Chuck. Maybe he is setting all this up to scare us."

Everyone was now looking at Chuck and waiting for a response. A big practical joke would be a better and more believable solution to what was going on. He was usually the big joker of the group but unfortunately even he couldn't pull off something this elaborate.

"Seriously? You think I set all this up just to pull a practical joke on you guys? I truly wish I could say that that's all this is. One big well planned, carefully thought out and perfectly timed joke. But it's not. None of this is a joke. It is really happening. I don't know why or how. But it is." Chuck was reluctant to continue but he did. "Ask away. I will answer what I can but honestly you probably won't believe me. Hell, I still don't believe it entirely."

Christy came to his defense, "You don't have to explain anything. I believe you and I have seen how, what's been going on, has been taking a toll on you."

"Of course, here comes Christy to defend him." Gloria now laying into Christy, "Like a love struck puppy. For all we know, you're in on it too. This is ridiculous. What the hell is going ...."

“The picture was taken in 1850. Right after they were married, this restaurant was the first place they had dinner as husband and wife.” Chuck looked up at the manager who nodded verifying what he had just said. “Thank you,” Chuck said to the manager as a hint to go ahead and leave them at the table. “Not long after the marriage they, we, had a daughter. Her name was Chloe. She was beautiful with golden blonde hair and hazel eyes.” His eyes had watered up. “Chloe got really sick and none of the doctors we brought in could figure out why. She was only four years old when she died.” He paused but couldn't gather himself, “I'm sorry. I'll finish this later.” He got up from the table, walked outside and just sat in the car with tears rolling down his face.

They all just sat there in silence. No one knew what to say or what to think about Chuck's story. The waiter came back with their drinks and asked if Chuck would be returning to join them. Steven was the first to answer, “Yes he will be. I'll go talk to him.”

Steven had gotten up and went outside to look for his cousin. He saw him in the rental with the door open. Just sitting there. “Hey cuz. You ok?”

Chuck looked up at Steven, his eyes were red, he had a look of defeat and exhaustion. "No. Not really. But I will be, hopefully." He chuckled and half smiled at his cousin. "I know this is a lot to hear or understand but I really am just as lost as the rest of you guys. I don't have any clue how to deal with all this cuz." Chuck just sat there staring at Steven, hoping for some words of wisdom or a joke. "I guess we better get back in there. Don't want to waste free food."

"That's the spirit. Oh shit, wait, bad choice of words. Ah hell. Let's just go eat." He tried to make a joke but kinda just stumbled over himself. "My bad cuz."

"It's OK. Not much I can do about that one. But I definitely need a drink." Chuck smiled at the thought of a cold beer and some hot food. Hopefully it would be enough to clear his mind and he was hoping that no one would ask any more questions.

"Before we head back in, I need to tell you something. Gloria and I are ummm, we're kinda dating. I know you two have been butting heads while we've been on this lil road trip but I wanted to tell you before we tell the girls. It happened a few months ago, we had dinner and that led to an amazing kiss and yeah."

“I had no idea, you guys hid it pretty damn good.” Chuck chuckled. “Hey, no worries cuz. If you're happy then I'm happy for you.” Chuck made his cousin smile with that, did a half handshake hug and started heading back to the girls.

While the guys were outside, the girls were getting into a heated argument at the table. Gloria was continuing about how she thought Chuck was making all the dream stuff up and wasn't being honest with them.

“How can you guys believe him? Christy you're smarter than this, something is seriously not right with him and I don't want you getting hurt. Doesn't this story or whatever it is seem crazy to anyone else? Come Harper, back me up here.”

“Gloria, why are you so set on making Chuck look like a psycho? Yes it does seem far fetched but he's our friend. Maybe there is some underlying trauma or maybe he took some bad drugs and he's having hallucinations.” Harper was trying to use her psychology background to try and make some sense of this situation. “Plus, why do you keep jumping down Christy's throat for sticking up for Chuck. She's being a good friend and yes, we know they like each other but he needs our support not to be treated like a psych patient."

"Finally, someone is trying to be the voice of reason. Yes, I do like Chuck. To be honest I love him and this is all very scary and overwhelming. But, Gloria, if you were sitting with him when that hand print just appeared on his neck or felt him shaking like he was having a seizure, you would have a different opinion." Christy was getting emotional thinking about the events of the past couple of days. "I don't know what to believe at this point but I do know that I don't plan on giving up on him. I won't abandon him when he needs us." The love and dedication Christy spoke with was inspiring to her friends.

"OK. Fine. I'll give him the benefit of the doubt but if this gets out of hand or violent we're taking him to a hospital or something." Gloria wanted to make sure her friends understood that she did care about Chuck but she wasn't willing to take any unnecessary risks.

"Agreed." Said Harper.

"OK. I can agree with that. But I think we need to let Steven know about this. It'll take the four of us working together, if it comes to the point where we need to take drastic measures. And it has to be the absolute last possible solution because if we have to go with it, Chuck won't trust any of us afterwards." Losing his trust was the worst part to Christy. They've been so close for so long she couldn't bear that thought. "If he is having some kind of psychotic break then we will get him the proper help he needs, not just some rinky dinky looney bin."

"I'll talk to Steven about it later." Gloria surprised the others by wanting to be the one to tell him. "He'll probably respond better to it from me anyways."

Confused, Harper asked "Why?"

"Well…. Umm… we're kinda dating." Gloria smiled mischievously. "It happened a few months ago, we met up for dinner and ended up kissing after we ate."

Christy was shocked but amused by the news. "So that's why you were so quick to snap at Chuck. You thought you were protecting Steven from his own cousin. That's funny!"

"Glo, why did you hide that from me? We're twins, we don't hide stuff from each other." Harper was slightly upset with her sister's hidden secret. "I mean I'm happy for you but you shoulda told me."

“Whoa whoa hold on a minute here. One, Christy, what's so funny about that? You've snapped at me just as bad or worse in the damned car. And Harper, I wanted to tell you, but Steve asked me to wait for a bit so we could both tell you.” Gloria was a bit annoyed with her sister and Christy. Especially Christy's remark about snapping on Chuck.

“It's funny because we're both doing the same thing and getting pissed at each other for it. Clearly we both care about each other and for the guys. We should be working together to help them, not opposing each other.” Christy tried to make her friends see how they were going about the situation all wrong.

“Glo, I get it but no more secrets. Jerk.” Harper said while smiling at her sister.

“OK Christy. I see what you're saying and I agree to work with you. But if it comes down to having to side with Chuck or Steve, I'm siding with Steve. I just want to be upfront with you cuz I know you're gonna still side with Chuck no matter what.” Gloria was going to do her best to be neutral and work to help both of the guys but made her final intentions clear to her friend.

“Understood. Though now we have a new problem.” Christy caught the sisters off guard with her statement. As they both looked at her intensely she said “Now we have to find Harper a guy friend.” They all laughed at her comment.

As Chuck and Steven approached the table they looked at each other then at the girls confused as to why they were laughing. Steven sat at the end of the table next to Gloria and Chuck sat across from him next to Christy.

“So, what's so funny? Not that I'm complaining, I'm glad to see a more cheerful atmosphere.” Steven was the first to break the silence. He looked at Gloria and nudged her with his shoulder.

Gloria whispered to Steven, “Well, Christy and Harper know about us. I'll let you break the news to your cousin.”

“Yeah, about that, he already knows. I told him when we were outside just now. So, since everyone knows our dirty little secret, SURPRISE.” Everyone laughed except for Gloria. She was giving Steven a dirty look. “Uh oh. What did I do?”

“Why does it have to be a dirty little secret?” Gloria was confused and a tad annoyed with Steven for that comment.

“Oh, come on babe, it's a joke. It's the title of a song, a good song actually by The All American Rejects. You know me and music, I use it in almost everything.” Steven was worried that he actually offended Gloria.

After a brief moment of silence and Gloria just looking at Steven, she started laughing. “I know dork, I just wanted to mess with you. I think you started to sweat a little bit.”

“Damn. Yeah you got me. That was just mean, well done babe.” Steven was smiling at her and she was smirking knowing that she played a good joke on him.

“Well, I don't know about the rest of you guys but I could definitely go for a drink.” Chuck smiled as he waived the waiter over. “Can we get a round of drinks please. Two draft beers and three vodka and cranberries.”

“Got it. Any appetizers? The breaded mushrooms and mozzarella sticks are really good.”

Everyone nodded yes and the waiter left to go put in their order. Within a couple minutes he was back with their drinks. And took their dinner order. Chuck and Steven ordered mushroom burgers, Christy ordered a BLT, Harper and Gloria ordered a double bacon cheeseburger. They planned on cutting it in half and splitting it, something they've always done since they were kids.

As they ate their dinner, Chuck started feeling a bit light headed. He had forgotten that he had taken the stay awake pills not long ago and the beer was starting to mix with them. He was starting to look flush and Gloria and Harper noticed first.

"Chuck, are you feeling ok? Your face is turning red. You look like a tomato." Harper asked with concern in her voice.

"Yeah, just the beer hitting me quick. I didn't eat very much today so it's got me feeling like a lightweight." He tried to laugh to throw off their concern. He waved to the waiter and asked for a big glass of ice cold water. "I'll be fine. No more beer for me though, I'll stick to water." He reassured the group and their expressions seem to light up a bit.

Surprising the others, Harper was the one to bring up the picture again. “I'm sorry but I have to ask, Chuck, what happened with the guy and the woman in the picture. I mean they both look so happy and in love.”

Chuck sighed, he had been hoping no one would bring up the picture again. “They were for a while but happy enough to have a daughter and love her for the rest of their lives. But the woman, Cassandra, had a very dark secret and she hurt someone very close to him. She thought he replaced their daughter with someone who she believed was unworthy of her husband's love and attention. All I can remember, at the moment, was that she made a decision to kill the boy. A boy that he swore to protect because the boy's father died saving him.” Chuck gave the short version of the story because he was still feeling light headed. “Honestly I can not remember anything else right now. It kinda hits me in bits and flashes.”

“That's one hell of a cliffhanger cuz. Guys why don't we call it a night. I'm pooped from all the driving and fresh air.” Steven was trying to give Chuck a break from the nightmare or memories. He could tell his cousin needed some sleep.

They tried to pay the bill but the waiter refused their money. So, as they left, they each put a twenty on the table leaving the waiter with a hundred dollar tip. They hurried out so he couldn't refuse the tip.

There was a small hotel not far from the restaurant where they got two rooms. Harper, Gloria and Steven shared one since it had two queen size beds. Chuck and Christy shared the other room with the single queen bed. Though Chuck was more concerned with Cassandra returning so he didn't plan on sleeping very much, if at all.

Chapter Four

Chuck refused to go to sleep, he knew that if he did, he would have a visit from HER. That was something he was trying his hardest to avoid. He also knew he couldn't continue on with the stay awake pills. After being up long enough, they would stop working and he wouldn't have any choice but to sleep. He had looked up possible issues with overuse of the pills and it mentioned psychosis and hallucinations. Meaning he would be seeing her whether he was awake or asleep. Chuck knew he could probably get another 12 to 13 hours of no sleep before things started to get bad.

He decided he was going to go for a drive, luckily he had the second set of keys to the rental. He climbed into the rental, turned the music to the local country station and began his little solo road trip. He passed the restaurant from earlier, wishing they had never stopped there or even took the route they did. He kept on driving, he didn't even need the GPS, he knew exactly where he was going. He was going home. He drove until his old house came into view. He drove up to the front door and put it in park. As he stepped out he felt an ominous presence in the atmosphere.

He walked up to the front door, knowing it would be locked, he tried to open it with no success. He stepped back and remembered that a key used to be hidden in a makeshift pocket under the main windows. He walked over to the window and sure enough, the key slid out and into his hand. A chill ran down his spine and he walked back to the front door. With the key he found, he inserted it into the lock and heard a click. The door opened with a haunting creak that echoed in the dark.

Chuck stepped inside and walked over to the sitting room. Over the fireplace was a picture of Charles and Cassandra. They had it painted shortly after their wedding. It was worn and covered with dust. The fireplace itself had ashes in the firebox as if it had been used recently. He knelt down, put in new logs and with the matches next to the wood basket he lit a fire. The orange glow spread across the room like golden tendrils. He walked to the center of the room and surveyed the scene as memories of how it used to look flashed in his mind. He saw the wedding party in the main room, all the people who came to see them wed.

As he stepped forward, reality set in and the room was dim again with only the glow of the fire lighting his way. He moved to the steps, imagining his old self carrying his new bride up the stairs to their room. He followed the memory, step for step, until he stopped outside the door to his old room. As he lifted his hand to reach for the doorknob, he noticed his hand was shaking. "Come on Chuck, get your shit together." Whether it was fear or the cold draft that caused the shake, he tried to give himself the courage to walk through the door.

He took a deep breath, held it for a moment and he opened the door. He took out his phone and turned on the flashlight. The small light illuminated the room like the glow from a full moon. He walked over to the bigger dresser on the left side of the room. Empty decanters and glasses rested on the dust covered dresser top. He opened the drawers, expecting them to be empty, he saw clothes that were centuries old. His old clothes. He rummaged through the drawers and in the back of the lowest drawer he found a piece of cloth. It was stained red and looked as if it had been torn from something bigger like a shirt or a dress. He remembered that Cassandra had a tear in her dress on the night they found Jacob's body.

He placed the stained cloth into his pocket and moved on to the next dresser. It was half the size of the main one and also cloaked in dust. Clearly no one had been there in a very long time. He again searched through the dresser but only found more clothes. On top of the dresser was an old writing tool, with a type of notebook. The inkwell had dried up and the glass was tinted from the old ink. Chuck grabbed the notebook and skimmed through it. It was a journal, it told about Charles's travels to Wills and Brooks, his wedding, Chloe's time alive and her death. He stopped for a moment to wipe away the tears gathering in his eyes. As he was about to continue reading he was interrupted by the creaking of the wood in the hallway.

He closed the book and put it under his arm so he could finish reading it later. He crept into the hallway to see what made the wood creak. Perhaps it was just the wind on some old floorboards. He stepped out of the room in time to see something moving in the dark towards a room at the end of the hall. He rushed down the hall to the room where he saw the figure. He opened the door to see someone standing at the window.

He stepped inside the room and slowly moved the light from the floor to the figure. As the light climbed, the dark figure moved to the opposite side of the room and spoke to him.

"Hello old friend. It's been quite a long time. I ask that you keep your light to the floor." His voice sounded like that of a young man's voice. "Is it strange being in a home that you've never lived in yourself? I'm sure the familiarity is both comforting and disturbing."

"That's one way of putting it. How do we know one another? Your voice is familiar but I can't quite figure it out." Chuck was oddly calm while speaking to the shadowy figure. "I assume you know the umm… the former me? Which, honestly, is one of the weirdest things I've ever said to a person."

"That is correct. I knew you when you lived in this house. When Chloe tragically passed and while you were married to that monster of a wife. I learned of her true self in a very unfortunate and painful way. I was the object of her revenge towards you after Chloe died. You were kind, caring and you treated me like a son."

At that very moment, Chuck knew who the shadowy figure that was lurking inside his old house was. "Jacob!!" He yelled out in disbelief and joy. He bolted towards the boy and threw his arms around him, as if hugging a long lost relative. "How are you here?

Jacob returned Chuck's hug and smiled. "Yes, it is me. Like I said, I learned of Cassandra's true self the hard way. I'm guessing not all of those memories have returned." Jacob chuckled. "It's still strange to me that you are both Charles and the man standing before me. I haven't seen anything like this in the entire time I've been alive."

"That makes two of us. I have no idea why this is happening or how it's happening. All I know is she's haunting my dreams and I feel like she's capable of killing me in them. I haven't slept in a couple of days. It's driving me insane and my friends think I am insane." Chuck could see a look of horror on Jacob's face.

"What do you mean she's haunting your dreams? She's alive? There's no way, it is impossible." Jacob was panicking and anger was beginning to fill the boy.

"Why is it not possible? You're here because of her curse, why would it be any different for her? She's clearly very powerful." Chuck was confused and was curious about what Jacob said.

"It's impossible because you had handled the problem with her before you died, in the past. You said you had a plan and a place that no one knew or could know about. You asked me to stay hidden from her and to keep my distance so she couldn't use me against you. So, I did as you asked. The last time I saw you was when you had come back from completing whatever plan you had put into motion. You had been gone for a few days and you said that it was done. You made sure everyone would be safe." Jacob was getting emotional. Even though Chuck had Charles's memories, Jacob remembers his friend's death, being buried and grieving over him.

"I'm sorry Jacob. I can't imagine how hard that was or even how difficult this all may be. I hate to ask but is there anything else that you can remember that may help me? She is powerful when she's only in my dreams. If she were to truly come after me in person I don't have any idea what I could do to protect myself or my family and friends. We are currently on vacation and headed to an island for sunshine and fun. This was definitely not on the brochure." Chuck tried to laugh but all that came out was an exhausted sigh.

"I'll help as much as I can. But I don't know all of the plans you had for her back then. I can confirm that we did not share a connection because she never came after me and before you.. Charles had passed, it was confirmed that

Cassandra never knew I was still alive." Jacob was glad to be able to help Chuck. He felt it was a way he could honor Charles and his father.

"Jacob, I truly appreciate your willingness to help. I know you don't know the people I'm traveling with but they are good people and I love them. Perhaps we can find a way that you can join us. There's strength in numbers and you are family to me just like they are. I do need to get back before anyone realizes that I'm gone. Do you have a cell phone?" Chuck thought it was a dumb question but he had to ask.

Jacob laughed. "Yes. I have a cell phone. Just because I'm old doesn't mean I haven't kept up with the times. I even have Facebook and I listen to Spotify. Here is my number, text me with the details and I will be nearby at all times. Though for obvious reasons, I do have to travel at night."

"Thank you. I will keep you posted on and message you as we go. We'll figure out how to add you to the vacation group and you will join us soon." Chuck hugged Jacob again and just looked at him. "It's so good to see you, Jacob."

"You as well my old friend. I look forward to your texts. See you soon…. Chuck. That'll take some getting used to." Jacob laughed.

As Chuck made his way back to the stairs he passed Chloe's room. He stopped in the doorway for a brief moment and reluctantly went in. He looked around the room with tears in his eyes. Though he personally had never been in there, in his lifetime, his mind remembered every single detail. Her small frame bed that he had made just for her, it had engravings of angels and flying horses. In the corner was her wooden rocking chair that she would spend hours on. Her closet with all her dresses that now looked old and weathered. Sitting on her bed was her absolute most favorite toy, her rag doll that she named Lizzy. They never knew where she got the name from but Chloe loved that doll so much. Chuck just sat on the edge of the bed with tears rolling down his face. As he left her room he noticed he still had the doll in his hand. He kept it and proceeded to walk out of the house, locking the door on the way out.

As he drove back to the hotel, Chuck took another pill and washed it down with water. He wasn't sure whose water bottle it was but thankfully it was still cold. The drive back felt different to him. He wasn't sure if it was because he finally knew he wasn't crazy. With Jacob, by some miracle or curse, now here looking out for him from the shadows as he should have done so many years ago. Chuck felt a small sense of relief. But now that he knows about Jacob, does that mean she does too?

Chuck pulled into the same parking space that they used when they arrived. He had hoped that no one would notice he had left. As he walked to the door to the room, Christy opened it with a look of concern and fear in her eyes.

"Where were you? I woke up a little bit ago and you were gone. I was about to wake the others when I saw you pulling in the parking lot. I was afraid something horrible had happened." She stood there with tears in her eyes.

Chuck felt awful that he had scared her so badly. But he was conflicted, should he tell her about Jacob and the house or keep his presence a secret. He finally had someone to corroborate his mad and terrifying story but would it only make things worse?

"I'm really sorry I scared you, that was not my intention. I needed to go for a drive and clear my head. I drove to the big house we passed on the way here." Chuck decided to only give her the half truth. Jacob was far too important to reveal that he was alive and his current condition.

"What? Why would you go there? Don't get me wrong, it's an amazing house and so big. But I don't understand why you drove all the way back to it." Confused by Chuck's confession. Christy's mind was racing with horrible thoughts. Was she there? Did Cassandra find a way to resurrect herself? Was he bitten? She wasn't even sure she believed in the whole vampire idea.

"Well, to add to the craziness of everything, that was my old house. I owned it in the 1850s. I know that sounds as crazy as everything else but it is true. I even somehow knew where a key was hidden. I went in and kinda just wandered around." He looked down as he pulled something from his back pocket. "This was Chloe's baby doll, she named her Lizzy." He handed the doll to Christy.

Christy took the doll as she moved aside for Chuck to enter the room. She looked at it, easily able to tell that this was an extremely old doll. She watched Chuck sit on the bed and smile at her as she held the doll.

“That was her favorite toy. I or Charles, whichever sounds less crazy. Gave it to her for her third birthday. She took it everywhere, she ate with it and even bathed with it.” He laughed a little as he thought about Chloe playing with her doll while she was getting a bath. “I couldn't stand the thought of leaving it in that cold empty ghost of a house.”

Christy just walked up to Chuck and hugged him. She didn't know what to say to him. How do you console someone who is grieving the death of someone they never knew, even though in some strange way he did know her. “I'm so sorry.” Was all she could think of saying. They just sat there, Chuck in her arms as she tried to understand what was happening.

“Thank you. I know this is weird and well… actually it's just weird. But you should get some sleep. I'm not tired but I will lay here with you. I don't have any other unexpected drives planned. Though if it's ok, I'll probably just turn on the TV.” Chuck clicked the remote on and found a channel playing country music videos. “If a good song comes on I'll try my best not to scare you with my singing.” Chuck was trying to bring some humor to the bleak situation.

Christy giggled, “Sing all you want, I don't mind listening to you sing.” She cuddled up in his arms with her head on his chest as he pulled the blanket up to keep them both warm.

Christy dozed off quickly as the music played. Chuck sang quietly along to a couple songs but as hard as he tried he ended up falling asleep.

There he was again on that same beach. A full moon in the sky lighting up everything around him. Something was different this time, it was oddly peaceful. As he surveyed the area he stopped when he noticed that the water was calm. There were no sounds of waves crashing into the shore, no sounds of seagulls squawking in the distance, nothing at all. He began walking, waiting for her to appear or strike. He had no idea what to expect from Cassandra.

Cassandra was stalking Chuck, like a cat stalking a mouse. She watched him roam along the sand. She knew he was looking for her but she was enjoying the fact that he was afraid of her. She moved along the trees keeping out of his sight and just watched him. She never thought that this day would come, that the man she once loved would be reborn. She had been wandering for so long, lost and feeling alone. But now, here he was. Within her grasp yet still so incredibly out of reach.

Chuck found some large logs that were in somewhat of a circle positioned around what looked like an old bonfire. They weren't far from the water, maybe twenty feet away. He was wishing he could start a fire when, coincidentally, he noticed someone matches laying in the sand next to his feet. “Of course there are matches. Why not?” He said aloud as he knelt down to pick them up and struck one to start the fire.

In a matter of minutes, he had the firing going and was enjoying the heat. As he looked out across the water, he could see the moon reflecting perfectly as if it was above a mirror. The stars in the sky stretched far and wide, he noticed Orion's belt, the dippers and even a shooting star. Everything was incredible until he noticed someone sitting across from him. “About time you showed up.” He wasn't surprised by her presence this time.

Amused by Chuck, Cassandra just smiled. The smile quickly turned into a look of content. “I was contemplating on if I should show myself or allow you a sense of false hope that maybe I was all just a figment of your imagination. Though I'm glad I decided to come sit. I can see you visited our home and even took a souvenir. Sweet little Lizzy, I have seen her in so long."

Chuck was doing his best to keep Jacob hidden in his mind. To keep him a secret from her for as long as possible. So, he just kept thinking about Chloe, maybe her memory would cloud Cassandra's emotions and keep her distracted.

"Yes, I went home. When we drove past it, I could see it as it once was and not as it is now. A home that reminds me of you, once full of love but has turned into a cold and hollow empty shell. Kind of ironic, isn't it, how someone can be so similar to a thing." He knew that would strike a nerve but he had to do whatever he could to keep Jacob safe.

"A cold and hollow empty shell am I? You're right, that is all that remains of me, for now. But you should know something, my beloved, you made me this way. Before Chloe died and I dealt with your little pet, even before you. I lived for years without the need for vengeance. A need that you created inside of me. I gave you the chance to become something more, something powerful and a chance to share our love forever."

“You're joking right? You offered to turn me, or past me, into a vampire? How exactly did that go?”

Cassandra could tell he was intrigued by what she just told him. She told him about the night that Charles had a taste of her power. She may have exaggerated his description of how he felt but as she continued she could see something in Chuck's eyes that was different from her late husband's. “Is this something that interests you? The thought of becoming a vampire?”

Chuck wasn't sure how to respond, “All my life I've had a strange fascination with vampires. I've seen so many vampire movies and read books about the subject but it was never real. It was always just a fantasy to see how it felt to become one of the most feared creatures in the history of monster movies.” He wasn't sure why he was telling her this. Was it to keep her preoccupied til he could wake up or was his inner dark secrets spilling out into his dream world with her?

“Hmm, isn't this an interesting discovery? Perhaps I met the wrong version of you in the wrong era. I thought Charles was going to give into the power offered to him but I believe he was too afraid of it. The idea of feeding on human blood and having to hunt for his meal seemed to be very off putting for him. But you, now you don't seem to be troubled by that idea. How does the proposition of living forever sit with you?" She was truly enjoying this conversation.

"Honestly? I like the idea very much. The thought of dying scares the shit out of me. It seriously gives me panic attacks when I am laying down and my mind wanders to that. Totally freaks me out. I have to turn the TV on or put on music to distract my damn brain." Chuck was definitely over sharing with her but he just couldn't help it.

"What if I could offer you the same deal I gave him all those years ago? Would you take it or would you throw it in my face and cast me aside as he did? Would you spend eternity with me, living as a god amongst mortals?" She watched him, from across the fire, as he sat there staring into the fire. She could see that he was truly thinking about her offer.

"What's the catch? I'm not gonna lie, I've thought about this long before you invaded my head. But…" He stopped himself and wondered what he was doing. Was he really debating, with the woman who had been torturing him these past few days, on joining her as a vampire?

“I could give you a sample of that life. Or as you say nowadays, a free trial. What do you say to that, my love?” She wasn't even sure if she could do that at this point but she wanted to know where his mind was on the matter.

“What? How could you even do that? Is that even possible?” He was shocked by her bold and ludicrous claim but at the same time he wondered if it was possible.

“Truly? I don't know.” Even she was surprised by her own honesty. “I know a small drop of my blood gave your other self my power, heightened senses and incredible strength. But I don't know how it would work in this setting. All you would need to do is kiss me.” She knew that by him kissing her, even in his head, he would be betraying his Christy.

“Kiss you? Why would I have to kiss you? From what you're saying all I need is a drop of your blood. Can't you just poke your finger or something?” He was caught off guard by the thought of kissing her. He wouldn't do that to Christy, she meant way too much to him and he wasn't going to jeopardize that.

“That's the only way it'll work. Though, again, I don't know if it'll even work since we are merely in your mind. My blood needs to be physically ingested in order for you to gain what I'm offering. The choice is yours. Either we kiss and see if you gain my gift or wake up and continue on your journey.” Cassandra was curious if she was strong enough to turn him while in his mind, though she did not think it was possible. She had noticed her anger towards Chuck was subsiding.

Chuck had really been considering her offer, which was starting to scare him. Could he really be that selfish and do that to Christy? After all they had been through and all she had done to show she had his back, how was he actually humoring this woman. “I don't think I can do it. I can't and won't betray Christy. I'm sorry. If things were different I might have said yes, but they're not.”

Cassandra's face went blank, like a stone statue. She just sat there, disappointment and anger began to build up in her. “I see you are just like him. Refusing a gift that would literally change your life and make it so much better. You are a fool just like he was. I suggest you leave before I remove your heart from your chest and eat it in front of you." She could feel her fangs growing and the anger deep inside was starting to take over.

Chuck got up, tripping over his feet as he tried to get around the logs. He didn't know where he was going but he knew he had to find a way to wake up fast. He briskly made his way up the beach from his original starting point. He could see her moving to the other side of the logs and she just glared at him.

Cassandra couldn't control her anger any longer. She ran after him, with the speed of a cheetah. Even with the sand being everywhere, under every step and stomp, she made a direct path for him. She would force the gift on him and see if he was more cooperative afterwards. As she reached him, she knocked him down in the sand, flipped him over onto his back, bit her lip and forced a kiss on him.

With that kiss her blood slipped into his tongue and rolled down his throat. He coughed and tried to spit it out and then his body went still. He started to convulse on the ground, like he was having a seizure. Then he stopped and just laid there in the sand. He noticed the stars were brighter just as everything went black.

When he opened his eyes, he saw Christy sitting next to him with that look of horror he was unfortunately becoming used to. He was happy to see her and so thankful that he actually woke up. But as she stared at him he remembered what just happened in his dream. He sat up and looked at her.

"What happened? What did you see?" He had hoped that he didn't talk in his sleep this time but had no idea what he may have done or said while he was out of it.

"Where to begin? You were mumbling most of the time, so I couldn't make out what you were saying. You did say you won't betray me. Which was sweet to hear but I only wish I knew what the conversation was. All of a sudden your body began to twitch then it turned into something seizure-like. I screamed for help but no one heard me. I was about to run out to get the others when you woke up." Christy was still sitting next to him and she couldn't help but notice how calm he was. Something about it just seemed off to her. "Care to explain?"

"I tried my best to not fall asleep but I couldn't help it. Like usual I woke up in dreamland and I was on the same beach but everything was off and eerily quiet." He looked down as he told her about the fire and Cassandra appearing and telling him about her offer to Charles. “She made me the same offer and that's when I said I wouldn't betray you. She tried to attack me and that's when I woke up. Maybe the force of hitting the sand is what woke me.” He knew he had just lied to her but if he told her about the kiss with the blood she would have freaked out. Maybe even try to make him go to the hospital, which he knew would not end well for him. “I'm ok though.”

“I am glad you're ok, but your body going into seizures like this can't be good.” She was concerned not only for his mental well-being but his physical one too. “Are you in any pain or hurting anywhere? I feel like this has to be taking a toll on you. You're not sleeping much and when you do, clearly it's not good restful sleep.”

“You're right it's not. I appreciate your concern but I think I'll be OK. Let's go get some breakfast, I'm so hungry I could eat a whole cow.” His joke, however lame, still made her smile. As he stood up, he pulled her closer and kissed her. He could hear both of their heart beats increasing. So, he pulled her in closer for another kiss.

As she stepped back, her face was flush and she was smiling like a kid on Christmas morning. “Wow. That was… just wow.” She smiled at Chuck and grabbed his hand. “Let's go get that breakfast. Maybe the others are up, they can join us and then we can get back on the road.”

Chuck smiled as they went to the others room and they all went down for breakfast. They all ate and packed up their stuff from the rooms. Steven went down to check them out and Chuck went for the luggage cart. He lost his balance when he reached out for the cart and he caught himself on the emergency exit door. His hand landed flat on the door and left a perfect indentation of his handprint in the metal of the door. He stopped and just looked at it, unable to explain how he was able to leave that deep of an indentation. That's when he remembered his dream and what she said about that drop of her blood. How was her blood able to affect him in the real world when it happened while he was asleep?

Once the car was loaded up. Chuck returned the cart. He could hear the housekeeping associate telling the manager what she had found on the door and was unable to explain it. Chuck smirked as he walked away to get in the rental. He felt stronger somehow and he liked it.

Chapter Five

Chuck's mind was racing at the fact that Cassandra's blood was able to have the effect that it did even when it happened in his dream. It made absolutely no sense to him, but it did increase his paranoia that maybe she could kill him in his dreams as well. As the rental made its way down the expressway, he thought back to his dream when she chased him down and pounced like a wild cat. Even then, when he tried to fight her off, she overpowered him and forced a tainted kiss on him. What if his former self had been bitten and the strength he felt at the hotel was laying there dormant. Had she turned him into a vampire before, but even if he was, how could those traits still be lingering around all these years later? Jacob never mentioned him getting bit and turning into a vampire. Maybe she just found a way to increase her strength over the years.

Charles must have thought he had succeeded in killing her all those years ago, but somehow she was able to cheat death and found a way to increase her powers. Which isn't that surprising considering how long it had been since those events had taken place. Even though Jacob seemed to be surprised at the fact that she was still alive, Chuck was thankful that he had agreed to help him. Part of him wondered if they were going to able to stop Cassandra and end her reign of terror, would Jacob return to being human. Chuck had seen so many vampire movies and he wasn't sure how much was true and how much was made up. Never in his wildest dreams did he ever expect vampires to be real, let alone chasing him and haunting his dreams. He had always wondered how it would feel to be a vampire and even what kind of vampire would he be. Would he turn into a bloodthirsty killer or would he be able to control himself.

Just then he felt a hand touch his shoulder causing him to jump about two inches off of his seat. “Holy shit!” He yelled as he looked at Christy's face, he could tell she wasn’t sure if she should be worried or laugh at the fact that she caught him off guard. He did her the favor of choosing for her and he started laughing. “I think you gave me a minor heart attack and I might need to check my shorts.” Everyone in the car started laughing at his comment and he could see the relief on Christy’s face. He knew that they all needed that laugh and he was happy to give it to them. Plus, it kind of got his mind off of the vampire thoughts.

Christy leaned towards Chuck, gave him a kiss and apologized for scaring him. “I really didn't mean to scare you like that. You seemed like you were off in space and I wanted to see if you were ok. You seem to be a bit distracted since we left the hotel, is there something on your mind?”

“I guess I was kinda spacing out. I was just thinking about the old house and the feel of it when I was there. It was like entering into a tomb, it was so cold, the air felt heavy and it felt so lonely. I got flashed of my past life while I was in the house and at one point that house was so full of life. Friends and family coming to visit, the house staff busy keeping up with the daily chores and the days before Chloe had passed. So many memories in that house and all that's left are its skin and bones. It's sad to think about and I never would have given it a thought if all this had not happened.” His voice has a depressed monotone sound as he spoke to Christy about his former residence.

“That sounds terribly lonely and depressing. I can’t imagine how you must feel with all these new but old memories. I don’t know how you're keeping it together so well, I would be an absolute mess by now. Is there anything else on your mind or any other crazy memories that you wanna talk about?" She was hoping that Chuck would say her and not any more crazy dreams.

"Well, there was this one thing that I can't quite get out of my head. And quite frankly it's all your fault." Chuck smiled at her mischievously as he leaned forward to kiss her. He knew what she was hinting at and there was no way he was going to tell her about his recent dream with Cassandra.

Christy smiled as she slowly sat back in her seat. "Just what I was hoping you would say. I've been thinking about us a lot recently and with the exception of the crazy dreams, I'm happy we're getting to spend this time together. When we get back home and back to the real world, I really hope we continue this journey together. I can definitely see a future with us together and so many amazingly fun new memories to make. And hopefully they can replace the old sad and scary ones." Her big smile softened a bit when she brought up his nightmarish memories.

"I would definitely like that. I won't lie, these dreams and memories have been absolutely insane. I would love to replace all of them with some amazing new ones with you. I think you are what's keeping me sane and not getting checked into the funny farm. I know some people who work at one and I've heard it's not so funny." Chuck laughed and smiled as he looked into Christy's eyes.

"I do come in handy sometimes. Plus, I don't think paper scrubs are a good look for you." She smirked, slowly looked into Chuck's eyes and pulled him closer to kiss him. "Plus, I've heard visitors aren't allowed to kiss the patients, so that's definitely a big no-no." She kissed him again, this time it was a slow deep kiss that took his breath away.

"Geez, will you two get a room already." Steven yelled from the front passenger side seat. "If you guys keep this up, I will be the one checking into the looney bin. Hey cuz, pass me a water while you're back there."

Chuck threw the water bottle at Steven. He was aiming for the back of his head but threw it a bit too hard. It hit the dash and bounced off the dash and hit him on the forehead. "Oops, my bad. I didn't mean to throw the bottle that hard, are you ok?" Chuck was trying his best not to laugh because it was honestly a good shot.

"Yeah whatever, dickhead. You're lucky Christy is sitting so close to you or I would whip this damn bottle back at you." Steven was rubbing his head from the ricocheted hit. He looked over at Gloria, he could see her silently giggling, so he opened the water bottle and dumped a few drops on her head. Her laughing turned into an irritated glare. “Awe what's the matter babe, you just looked so hot, I thought I'd help cool ya down.” Steven and Chuck were both laughing now.

“Oh yeah?” Gloria tapped the breaks of the rental hard enough to make Steven spill the entire water bottle all over his shirt and pants.

Everyone in the car was laughing so hard, Gloria had to pull the car over because she was almost in tears from laughing so hard. Even Steven, who was now soaked, was laughing. They sat there for a few minutes, mostly to let all the laughing subside but also because Steven wanted to get his towel from his bag so he could dry off. He didn't mind the damp clothes, after all it was summer time. Plus, with the sun beating down on him through the window, he knew his clothes would dry soon and until then it would keep him cool.

Steven got back into the passenger seat and smiled at Gloria. “Well played ma’am. That was nicely timed Glo, didn’t know you had it in ya. But… ummm…you do know this means war." Steven gave her a sinister smile then kissed her on the cheek.

"War? Don't start something you won't be able to finish sir." Gloria said with a crooked grin and a hint of sarcasm when she said "sir".

"You do know who I grew up with right? That guy back there was the king of pranks, he slowed down in high school but every now and then he reminds the family with some crazy off the wall prank. Hell, he even got suspended in middle school for a couple of them." Steven was smiling from ear to ear while talking about Chuck's antics.

"Hey cuz, stop giving away trade secrets. Now you're getting me involved and I don't know if anyone is ready for my sinister alter ego to make his triumphant return." Chuck already had a few ideas brewing in his head that would be hilarious, at least to him and Steven they would be.

"Why don't we make this truly a war, girls vs boys. We may have an extra person but if Chuck is as good as he thinks he is, then it shouldn't matter. All those who agree say "Hell yeah!"

Everyone in the car said “hell yeah” at the exact same time and started laughing.

“Sounds like it's on gentlemen. Maybe the best team win and the losers buy the drink for the first night when we get to the island.” Gloria upped the stakes to give everyone some proper motivation.

“Oh, this is gonna be good. I like free drinks and hopefully there are no sore losers.” Steven threw in some trash talk for the fun of it.

“I have a quick question, are there any rules or things that are off limits in this war? Or is it anything and everything goes?” Harper wanted some clarification on the terms of the game. She knew her sister talked a good game but she was also quick to get mad if something offended her.

“Good question Harper. I think we should ban anything life threatening or that would get us kicked out of a Hotel.” Christy threw that out there quickly because Chuck had told her about some of his past pranks and knew he could get a bit carried away when he was really into the planning.

Chuck looked at Christy, smiled at her and gave her a little wink. “Awww is someone getting nervous?” He chuckled. “I can agree to those limits if everyone else wants them.”

“Sounds good to me.” Gloria said as she gave Steven a side-eyed look.

“Yeah, I'm cool with that and just to add one last thing, no one is allowed to get seriously pissed off at anyone. It's just a game and we all care about each other, so let's not take anything personal or to heart.” Steven knew how Gloria's emotions were quick to flip flop on certain things.

“So, the game is on. Good luck boys, the girls will win this easily. Plus, science proved that us girls are smarter than you boys.” Gloria was starting her trash talking already.

Chuck texted Jacob, “I think I may have found a way to get you in with the group. Plus, I checked the flight times with my cousin and it's a night flight. I bought you a ticket, I'll send the link so you will be able to board with us.” Chuck cautiously glimpsed at Christy to make sure she wasn't watching him as he sent that text.

Jacob replied back, “Thank you for the ticket. I don't think I should join you all in the car since, as you know, sunlight is not my friend.” He added the laughing and sun emoji at the end of the text.

Chuck snickered as he read the text and saw the emojis. “I agree. Did you remember anything about the old me getting bit by Cassandra? I had a crazy dream where she forced a kiss on me and she got a drop of her blood in my mouth. I don't know how but it gave me some crazy strength but how is that possible if it happened in a dream?”

Jacob was shocked by Chuck's text, he replied to him “She's been in hiding all these years, who knows what she was able to learn in that time. Maybe she picked up some witchcraft and it was a spell. I honestly don't know how she was able to pull that off. I never knew the extent of her abilities. I did find out that the one who made her was extremely old and is still alive. I never found him but heard plenty of rumors over the years.”

“Wow. That's crazy and interesting. I wonder how old he is and what he is able to do. Anyways, I gotta get back to these goofballs. I'll text you again soon and with more info. Good luck!” Chuck added the thumbs up emoji to the text for fun. It was funny to him that he was texting a vampire over a hundred years old and using emojis.

Jacob replied with the thumbs up emoji as well and said "OK. Talk soon. Be safe my friend."

Chuck quickly texts Steven "So since you got me into this mess, do you have any ideas on what you wanna do?"

"Me? You're the king of the pranks. I was just hoping to follow you to free drinks and bragging rights lol."

"Oy vey. OK. I think we start small and work our way to a grand finale. Next rest stop we need to get some dragon snaps, a couple of coke, some mentos and some Vaseline. These will be our small to medium pranks. Grab Gloria's phone, she has an iPhone and we can switch the screens to android. I think I may be the only one with an android actually lol. I'll do it to Christy and Harper's phones while I'm sitting here. Oh, and since they're my ideas, you can buy the supplies." Chuck added the wink face emoji at the end of the text.

Steven replied back, "Deal. We just need to make sure the coke and mentos trick is done outside. It'll be a bitch to clean up in here and we wanna make sure we get our deposit back. I was thinking maybe putting peanut butter under the car door handles too. It'll gross them out and be fckn hilarious."

"Sounds good. But I'm not cleaning up any puke if they happen to get really grossed out. That's all you cuz." Chuck laughed as he texted Steven back. Christy looked over at him suspiciously.

"What are you up to mister? I see you texting away over there." Christy said with squinty eyes. "I can see those wheels of mischief turning, I'll be keeping an eye on you."

"Well, don't threaten me with a good time." Chuck leaned over to Christy and kissed her. "You know, you could be our double agent and help us win. I can guarantee your share of the victory spoils."

"You want me to turn on my besties, for some drinks that you'll probably buy me anyways? I think I'll pass, I'd much rather have the bragging rights over you." Christy smiled and winked at Chuck, she then gave him a little peck on the cheek and started texting Harper.

"So, we need to come up with something good. These boys are already plotting away over here and I know from first hand account that Chuck over here is quite the trickster." Christy had turned her phone away from Chuck to make sure he couldn't read his texts.

Harper replied with the surprise face emoji and said "I have a couple of ideas but it's just stuff I've seen on Facebook reels. Like the coke and mentos trick. I'll keep scouring the internet until I find something good. We will win this little war."

"I hope so lol I was asked to be a double agent and turned it down. Sistas before mistas right." Christy ended the text with the thumbs up and smiley emojis.

Chuck could hear Harper snickering in the seat in front of him. He smiled until he remembered that he hadn't taken one of his stay awake pills since yesterday. He was sitting too close to Christy to try and take one of the pills, plus the noise from the pill bottle would have been heard by Harper as well. He started to get a little bit nervous, he grabbed a pepsi from the cooler and chugged it. He let out a big burp that startled Christy. He laughed and apologized to everyone for the loud burp.

He took out his phone and started googling stuff about vampires in the 1850s. He wasn't sure if he'd find anything but he hoped that if he started reading something interesting it might just keep him awake. As he scrolled through the search results he saw a link to a site that talked about strange occurrences in history. He was shocked to see a sketch of a woman who closely resembled Cassandra, her eyes seemed younger than when he had seen them in his last dream. Her eyes were the eyes of someone yet to discover the horrors life had in store for her. When Chuck had his last run in with her, the night at the hotel, he could see something in her eyes that said she was no longer afraid of the horrors because she herself had become one of them. She had to learn the hard way and lost her innocence in the process. She became something dark and malevolent, the taker of others' innocence. In one swift moment she could end someone's life, but she could also curse them with an unforgiving and nightmarish existence. One that he had planned to find a way to end and freeJacob and himself from the clutches of her lethal ice cold grip.

As he read the article about her, he realized it painted her as the victim of an even older vampire who left a bloody note throughout history. Nothing had been found about the vampire who attacked her or if he was even still living. It said she had been attacked while staying at an INN after being accidentally separated from her family. It stated that after the attack she made her way home after being missing for five weeks. When she did return home, she did something unthinkable and horrendous, she killed her family. Chuck thought, "She must have blamed them for her attack or maybe she thought that if they had only looked for her none of this would have ever happened." The bodies of her family members had been ravaged and torn apart, since there were no police back then it must have been dismissed as an animal attack. As he scrolled down he noticed something that truly shook him to his core.

The next article spoke about an urban legend on the island that they were going to, it said the island was plagued by random deaths for the last hundred years or so. They all seemed to be centralized around a specific beach, unfortunately they did not name the beach and the article was never finished. The site mentioned how the writer of that article, TJ Holmes, was investigating the island and disappeared. A body was never found and no suspects were ever charged with a murder or anything. The site did however list that they had one picture that Holmes sent in, there was a ten dollar fee to see the picture but all proceeds went to Holmes's family.

Chuck was curious about the picture and he had no problem with paying the ten dollars. Luckily he had some money on his cashapp account, he clicked on the buy icon for the picture and paid. The site asked for his email address so they could send a receipt and the picture along with it. He got the email confirmation for the payment and the receipt, now he was waiting for the picture to arrive. After a few minutes he was starting to get annoyed, he looked up and saw Steven sleeping, Harper watching TikTok and Christy was reading Salem's Lot by Stephen King. Then his phone buzzed, the email popped up in his notification bar, Chuck swiped down and clicked on the Gmail icon. As the image loaded, Chuck could feel his heart beating faster. He felt both disappointed and relieved at the same time. The ten dollar picture was a blurry photo of a hand with a sapphire blue ring.

Chuck let out a nervous laugh as he continued to examine the picture, he did not recognize the ring or the hand. He was glad that it wasn't a picture of Cassandra, which is what and who he thought he was going to see. He had a feeling that Cassandra was somehow behind him finding that specific island and it made a lot of sense to him. He felt like it was a set up, the text message and the history of it, it all seemed too coincidental. He was still surprised by what he read about the island. Chuck had thought about telling the others what he found online but he quickly dismissed the thought. There was already enough craziness going on without adding that to it. He remembered Jacob mentioning that his past self said he had taken care of the "Cassandra problem" though the details were never shared. Maybe his solution wasn't quite as permanent as he thought it was.

Chuck was beginning to feel sleepy and he knew he had no chance of popping a stay awake pill while he was in the rental with everyone around him. The worst part was that he had drunk the last pepsi and there was nothing left with caffeine in the cooler. He could feel his eyelids getting heavier and knew that it was only a matter of moments before he would fall asleep. He had hoped that a rest stop was near but the sign on the side of the expressway said it was another ten miles. He went back to the website where he had found the picture and link about the island. He scrolled past the sketch of Cassandra, the link about Island and saw something that talked about children of vampires. He clicked on it and noticed something about human/vampire hybrid children. It said that sometimes the child of humans and vampires will die young, but it was only so that the body could acclimate to the emergence of the vampiric genes. It stated that the child will often be sick and that is usually due to the body trying to feed on its own blood, the vampire parent will recognize this and often need to feed the child their own blood due to it already containing the genes of the vampire. On most occasions it will seem as if the child dies, the body will put itself in something like a hibernation until it is fully accustomed to its new way of living. The child will then awaken, this can take anywhere from days to months or maybe even a year depending on the strength of the vampiric parent.

Chuck almost dropped his phone but was able to catch it quickly. He couldn't believe what he had just read. He remembered that many times Chloe would get sick and Cassandra would lock herself and Chloe away in Chloe's room. It never made sense to Charles, or in the memories Chuck was having, why she would do this but this article made perfect sense. Which was crazy considering the world did not appear to know of the existence of vampires, even Chuck thought they were just something made up for books, movies and tv shows. How could whomever owned this site know all of this or even have the ability to check if what was posted was facts or fiction. Chuck began scrolling down to the bottom of the site to see if any contact info or an email was listed. He had to know where and how they were getting this information.

At the very bottom of the screen there was a link to ask the site owners questions or to submit anything worth looking into. Chuck clicked on it, filled out the information boxes using a fake name and used an email address that he saved for video game apps when they needed to bind to something in order to save game progress. Chuck typed in the comments/questions box,

"Hello, I was wondering how you obtain your info. I really enjoyed the site and I am a huge fan of the supernatural. I had a friend who claimed he had a run in with a vampire recently and that when she kissed him, she slipped a drop of blood in with the kiss. My friend claimed he temporarily gained some super-human abilities like his strength increased, senses were super sensitive and he was able to run faster than a sports car. I told him it sounded like BS but he swore to me that it was true and that he planned on seeing this person who gave him the supposed abilities again. Am I wrong to doubt him or is it a true possibility? Also, I was wondering about the article regarding the children of humans and vampires. Is that a factual possibility? Thank you for your time."

He sent the message and now just had to wait for a reply.

Chuck quickly texts Jacob. “I need to ask you something, it's going to sound crazy but I need to know. Have you ever heard of a child that was born to the parents of a human and vampire going into some kind of hibernate state, after what seemed like death and coming back to life? Is that something true or possible? I just read something online, here's the link, and it's got me freaking out.”

He sent the message and was watching his phone like a hawk. He couldn't decide if he was scared or excited or just plain out of his mind. He was half tempted to let himself fall asleep and question Cassandra. But something inside him, something deep down, screamed at him to keep this from her. If for one tiny, miniscule chance that this was true and there was a possibility that Chloe could be alive somewhere, he had to hide this thought from her.

Jacob had finally messaged him back. “Honestly, I have no clue if what you found was true. I'm guessing you messaged the site administrator. I did the same too. I will ask around and see if anyone has heard of any truth to this. You'd be surprised how many vampires there are in the world, most are hard working family members. But as soon as I hear back I will message you. Be safe and try not to dwell on this."

"I will do my absolute best, but I can't guarantee it. It's so hard to imagine that she's been alive all this time and all alone. It breaks my heart." Chuck could feel the tears building up as he sent the text to Jacob.

"Believe me, I understand. It was quite lonely at first but after a while you learn to adapt and make friends. You build trust with people, spend your life doing good and do the best you can. We will find out the truth. Seems we have a lot of work to do in a short amount of time. I'll do what I can to see if there is any truth to that article. Also, keep in mind, you are supposed to be on vacation so you should try to enjoy yourself. It just might be the distraction you need." Jacobs' reply helped Chuck feel slightly better but he knew if Chuck was as similar to Charles as he thought he was, nothing short of the truth would ease his mind.

"I know you are right, but every time I try to relax Cassandra finds a way to mess with my head and now this. Plus, I'm still freaking out over her being able to give me that super strength, its effects only lasted for a short while but wow. OK, I know I need to stop because I am keeping myself from relaxing. I'm gonna have them pull off the expressway and stop at a Walmart or something." Chuck knew that they had to stop soon anyway for their prank supplies, some water, pops and chips for their ride to the airport. He also knew that it would be his last opportunity to take one of his stay awake pills so he could keep Cassandra away.

"Ok, sounds good. I'll let you know what I find and you do the same if the site admins message you back. Have some cool ranch doritos for me. We will talk soon." Jacob ended the chat with something he thought would be funny.

Chuck sat there for a minute looking out the window. He wondered how Chloe would look now and would she even see the resemblance between him and Charles. He snapped out of his daze when he noticed the Walmart sign in the distance, he called up to Gloria to get off on the next exit so they could make a quick supply run. He started making a list of stuff he wanted to pick up while at the store. He thought maybe he would get something for Christy to make her smile and show her how much he appreciated her. He remembered her mentioning the summer-halloween blankets that she had seen on tiktok or facebook. He'd pick out one of those and a nice card.

Once they parked and got inside the store, Chuck slipped off saying he had to use the restroom. He popped his stay awake pill and hid another in his pocket, he figured that would be smarter than trying to open a noisy bottle in the car. He threw the empty bottle away and began his shopping. He found her a blue blanket with skeletons in floaties and summer drinks in their boney hands, it was a pretty cool and funny design. He next found her a very heartwarming card and he knew that the moment she read it she would instantly smile. Next he went and picked out one of those big party poppers, he would hit those the moment they all got to the car. He quickly grabbed a few more prank items, a case of pepsi and a bag of cool ranch Doritos. He paid for the items and made his way to the car, since he had the spare key, he hid in the back where Christy and he were sitting. He waited for everyone else to start coming out, he texted Christy that he was in line and about to pay. He had the party popper aimed at the back hatch door. As soon as the back door was up all the way and he could see the girls, he twisted the popper, launching the confetti at them.

Harper, Gloria and Christy all jumped and screamed at the same time. The loud "pop" and the confetti launching at them scared them so bad that they dropped the bags they were carrying to the rental. Thankfully, none of them had bought anything breakable or in a glass container. Chuck was in the backseat laughing while the girls were still trying to catch their breath from the big boom. Chuck peeked over the seat to see them loading their stuff into the rental and giving him a dirty look at the same time. What they didn't notice was that Steven was by the cart corral behind them and he had been filming the entire time.

Chuck looked over at his cousin, "Did you get that recorded nicely? Send it to me when you get a chance, I definitely want to see that one. The timing was perfect and you three screaming at the exact same time was priceless." Chuck fell over in the backseat as he started laughing again.

"You know it cuz. I don't know how you guys didn't see me, I wasn't even hiding that well. I think this may be tiktok worthy or even instagram. I wonder how many likes we can get for this video. Hmmm…." Steven was tapping his chin in a thinking fashion. He had no actual intention of posting the video online, but it was fun teasing the girls with the idea.

"Steve, if that video makes it online, I can personally guarantee that you will regret it. Not only will you be sleeping on the floor, I will tell everyone you got crabs while we were on vacation and that you had to spend the whole time in the room so it wouldn't spread." Gloria gave him a sinister smile.

"What the hell? That's not even funny, it's just rude and evil. I wasn't actually going to post it, I would think you know me better than that by now and especially know when I am joking." Steven put his phone away, climbed into the driver seat and sat there waiting for everyone to be ready to head out. He wasn't actually mad but he was playing the part perfectly.

"Babe, I'm sorry, I was just kidding. I would never say or do anything like that to you. Please don't be mad at me." Gloria seriously thought she had pissed off Steven with her comments.

"Yeah, I know." Steven smiled at Gloria and winked. "I gotta at least pretend to be mad, though that was pretty evil on your part. Who knew you could stoop to such drastic and sadistic measures. I don't know if I should be proud or afraid, or a bit of both."

"I'd definitely go with a bit of both." Harper said from behind her sister's seat.

At the same time Chuck and Christy both said, “I agree.”

Gloria just smiled as everyone laughed at her and Steven's little conversation. “Well, I guess now you know not to mess with me, don’t ya.”

“I sure do.” Steven started the car and began backing out of the parking space. He hit the brakes abruptly when he saw something standing in the view of the backup camera. He quickly turned around in his seat to see who was standing behind the vehicle. He felt a chill run down his spine when there was no one standing behind them. “Please tell me someone else saw that too. There was someone standing behind the car, it was the torso of a lady in a white dress and she was on the uh.. backup camera.”

“Ha ha, nice try. There was no one behind us and you are not gonna scare us with some made-up BS.” Harper was the first to respond to Steven.

“No, I’m serious. There was a woman standing behind us as I started pulling out of the parking spot.” Steven was honestly freaking out because he could have sworn that there was a lady there on the screen.

“Is that why you slammed on the brakes? I didn’t see anything and I'm way back here but it's possible someone could have been running past the rental as you were backing up.” Christy could see the fear and confusion in Stevens' eyes.

“That's the thing, she wasn’t running. Whoever was out there was literally just standing there, not moving or anything. As soon as I turned around to look out the back window, she was gone.” Steven was sure he had seen the woman standing there behind the car, but how was she able to just disappear that quick.

“Well, whoever she was, she's gone now. Let's get this party rollin and get to the airport so we don't have to reschedule the flight and delay our island fun.” Chuck jumped in quickly to redirect the questioning and change the subject.

“Good idea cuz. See, you do come in handy every once in a while.” Steven knew that Chuck had intentionally spoken up to change the subject for him and get everyone's mind back on the road. He was grateful to his cousin for his quick thinking.

Steven continued backing out of the parking spot and made his way back to the expressway. He knew too much time had been taken on the conversation after the prank and his ghost encounter. He was still paranoid about what he had seen, every once in a while he would glimpse back through the rear view mirror to see if anyone who wasn't supposed to be there was there. He reached over to hold Gloria's hand while he drove, he meant it in a sweet way but it was also a way to keep him grounded. The last thing he needed was for his mind to start playing tricks on him. He wanted to leave the crazy stuff alone and to the professionals.

Chuck knew his cousin needed the rescue, but deep down he felt as if Cassandra had something to do with Stevens' strange experience. The chances of another paranormal being messing with them seemed extremely small and highly unlikely. The idea that she was responsible for what happened was much more plausible and made the most sense to him. There was a slight possibility that he was just quick to blame her since she was the one haunting him and preventing him from getting some real rest. So, there was possibly some biased thinking on his part.

Chuck heard a ping noise come from his phone. He knew it was the sound of his email alerting him that he had a new message. He had been waiting with anticipation for a reply from the administrator of the site where he found the information about Cassandra and the human/ vampire child cocoon theory. As he grabbed his phone, he could feel his heart begin to beat faster and anxiety increasing. He swiped down and it was an email from the administrator of the site.

The email said:

"Dear sir or Madam,

My name is CJ, I am the site creator and administrator. Thank you for your interest in my website and its articles. Usually, I get an unusual amount of requests for bigfoot or alien photos, but your questions were far from that. You had a very interesting and thought provoking question. Believe it or not, but I get a lot of my information from investigating strange occurrences. The investigations are done by myself or a respected member of my team, we never use any freelance writers. We do that to help prevent any fictitious articles and we strive to be thorough with each and every lead we take. Some may think we are just a bunch of crazies but I can swear that every article posted on my site is 100% true. Which is why

I found your email quite intriguing. Through the research done by myself and my team, I believe what happened to your “friend” is a for sure possibility.

I believe this is a possibility because the vampire's power is held within its blood. When a vampire turns a human they must first drain that person of their human blood, then the vampire has that person drink their blood which is what begins the transformation. The vampire's blood spreads throughout the body, basically changing the genetic makeup of the victim. This is what allows them to grow fangs, nails become talon-like, increased strength and senses and often they develop extra abilities. It's hard to list what they could be because the possibilities are infinite. Along with these abilities they will gain a regenerative system and their aging is slowed down tremendously, so a person can look twenty-five but actually be two hundred and twenty-five. As far as receiving temporary powers, it is possible since the receiving party has not had their blood drained, the body's natural immunity would fight and kill off the foreign entity inside of the body. The vampire's blood would be like an infection in the body, the white cells would treat the infection as such and eliminate it. It’s the body doing what it does best and protecting itself.

Now, personally, I would advise your "friend" to steer clear of this vampire, there is no guarantee that they actually plan on turning them. It could be a simple ploy to lure them somewhere where the vamp feels safe and then it's dinner time. Though not all vampires are untrustworthy, some are very upfront about their intentions and I've even heard of some offering to pay for fresh blood. Fast food for vamps. Sounds crazy but it's a more civil and humane way for them to live.

As far as the other article you asked about, the human/vampire child theory, yes I do believe it is possible. That was an investigation that I, myself, conducted. I can not reveal my source but I can say that the vampire/human child was a female, her parents had died before her transformation was completed and she was raised by a stranger who happened to find her. She was very lucky that he had found her when he did, he taught her everything she needed to know in order to survive. I believe she is still living somewhere in Tennessee, she is one of few hybrids that have been around since sometime in the late 1800s. She's changed her name several times over the years, which is a common thing amongst the vampire communities. She had been told the tragic story of her parents by this stranger. About how their love was built on a horrible lie and eventually led to the end of them both. She was reluctant to discuss further details and out of respect for her I did not continue the interview.

But as with all things, it is up to you to decide whether you believe in the impossible and the improbable or not. I appreciate you reaching out to me with your questions. I do hope I was able to help you and your "friend". I know it is a big step to be open-minded and not immediately dismiss the idea of the supernatural or, as some may say, the unholy. If you have any further questions, please feel free to send me an email.

Sincerely,

CJ"

Chapter Six

Chuck was astounded over the email he had received from the site owner. He knew for a fact that vampires existed, but not to the degree that she spoke about. There was so much he didn't know and understand that it made his situation with Cassandra that much scarier. He reached down into his pocket and took out the last of the stay awake pills that he had. It had been about four hours since they got back on the road. He forgot to buy more when they stopped at the store and loaded up on snacks and supplies. He grabbed a Pepsi and swallowed the pill without Christy or anyone else seeing him. He would have to fake needing a bathroom break to get them to make a stop at a gas station.

He looked at his phone and thought about messaging Jacob. His mind began to wonder, if the girl the site owner spoke about was Chloe, who could the stranger have been who had helped her? He assumed that if Jacob knew Chloe was still alive he would have told him, but technically he and Jacob only just met. There was probably still a level of uncertainty for Jacob regarding him and Charles. Even with memories from Charles and Cassandra stalking him, Jacob truly does not know Chuck. It had been decades, more like a couple of hundred years, since Jacob had seen Charles. Then to see him so much later as a younger man, in a whole different lifetime, it's been quite interesting for both men. Plus, with Cassandra being able to snoop around Chuck's mind, it was probably good that Chloe was never mentioned. Whether she's alive or not, her safety to Chuck is a top priority.

He was curious if she remembers Charles. Would she see him as her father or as a stranger? How would he feel if he were to see her? Would there be an instant father-daughter connection or would it be awkward? He had so many questions and scenarios playing in his mind. He was so distracted that he didn't even hear Christy calling his name. It wasn't until she smacked his arm, and startled him, did he snap back to reality and respond to her.

"Whoa. Hey. Sorry about that. What's up? Kinda sorta spaced out for a bit there." Chuck hadn't realized that Christy had been calling his name for the last few minutes.

"You ok? It was like you were frozen or something. I was calling you and calling you, finally gave up and just smacked your arm. Was it her again?" Christy looked at Chuck with concern.

"No, it wasn't Cassandra this time. I just spaced out while I was looking out the window. I promise I am ok." Chuck smiled at her in hopes of settling her nerves a bit. "To be honest, I was thinking about us having our first real date when we get to the island. Just you and me, a nice romantic dinner and hopefully a clear star filled night." He knew that would get her mind off of his little space out episode.

"That sounds absolutely amazing and I can not wait. I may have bought a dress when we stopped earlier and I think you'll like it." Christy was smiling from ear to ear.

"I'm sure you are going to look incredibly gorgeous and I am so looking forward to spending some time with you. Especially outside of this car, so we can stretch our legs and maybe dance around." Chuck was really looking forward to an evening with Christy without their friends. Chuck appreciated and cared about them all but the last couple of days had been a bit cramped.

"Cuz you know you can't dance. You are way to white and you barely have two left feet. That's a train wreck waiting to happen." Steven yelled to Chuck from the front seat.

"Whatever jackass. I can probably dance better than you. How are you Mexican and you have no rhythm? You're so bad you can't even shake a salt shaker." Chuck had everyone in the car laughing, including his cousin.

"Ok ok. I'll admit that was a good one." Steven was too busy laughing to even try to make a comment back to Chuck.

Gloria looked at Steven. "Damn babe, can't even try to make a decent comeback? Lame. How are you guys gonna win this bet if you can't even talk some good shit to your own cousin." Gloria was hoping she could turn Steven against Chuck so the girls could win the bet.

"You're gonna have to try harder than that Glo. Chuck and I have been talking shit for a very long time, so it won't be that easy to turn us against each other." Steven knew exactly what she was up to and he smiled at her.

"If I was really trying, you would know it. And believe me, you would side with me if you knew what was good for ya." Gloria got a little cocky figuring she could easily get Steven to double cross his cousin, if she truly wanted him too. Afterall, what guy is going to deny his girlfriend a victory if she properly motivates him.

“Oh really, you think so? Then what's to stop Chuck from trying to get Christy to do the same? Or for fun, what makes you think I won’t secretly help Chuck win, while I have you thinking you have the upper hand.” Steven was just having fun messing with Gloria.

“FINE!! Whatever. Just take my fun away. Just remember something, mister I’m sticking with my cousin,” she quickly flashed her breast at Steven while he was driving, “I have those and he doesn’t”

“Gloria you weirdo, keep those put away. No one wants to see them flapping around like that.” Harper was shocked by her sister flashing Steven.

“Well, I wouldn't say no one.” Steven said with a mischievous grin.

“That's what I thought. Keep that or those in mind.” Gloria said while smiling as she went back to playing on her phone.

“I definitely didn’t see that one coming. I guess the stakes are higher on this bet than we anticipated.” Chuck said while laughing from the back seat. “Hey, if we can stop at the next gas station, I would really appreciate it. I gotta pee like a damn race horse.”

“What the hell cuz, you have the bladder of a five year old. I think there is one coming up pretty soon but you better be quick, we’re on a tight schedule.” Steven knew they had spent too much time at the hotel and at the store. They needed to get to the airport so he wouldn’t have to try and reschedule things again.

“I’ll be quick. Scouts honor!” Chuck replied.

“Everyone here knows you weren’t a boy scout. The closest thing to you being any kind of scout is those boxes of girl scout cookies that you buy for your mom and Christy.” Steven was giving his cousin a hard time but it got some laughs from everyone in the car. He looked over at Gloria and said, “Is that more to your liking babe?”

Gloria laughed, “Yeah, that is definitely better. I knew you had a pair somewhere down there.”

“Damn cuz, I didn't know you brought your leash on vacations. Does it match her purse, you know the one where she usually keeps your balls in?” Chuck taunted his cousin, he was hoping to see if he would keep their banter going.

“They do match but usually we keep the leash for the kinky bedroom stuff and they’re in her purse because they are so big they make my back hurt having to carry them all the time.” Steven gave into Chuck's taunts. “I know you get jealous sometimes since you have them tiny stones. I don’t know how you ever kept a girlfriend, though they do say women love to laugh so maybe that's it?”

Chuck laughed at his cousin's words. “Clearly Glo has let you use them for vacation, it appears you are using them well and not just sitting on them or using them for decorations.”

“Keep it up and we won’t be stopping at that gas station.” Steven had run out of things to come back with when he saw the sign saying the next rest stop was coming up in a mile.

Little did everyone know that Chuck's reason for needing to stop had nothing to do with the bathroom. He needed those stay awake pills desperately, it was the only way he knew he could keep Cassandra away. At least until the pills stopped working. After that point he had no idea what he was going to do, perhaps Jacob would have some information for him by then. If not, then Cassandra would be back to haunting his dreams and doing whatever she had planned for him.

"Alright alright. I will take a break from the shit talking. For now." Chuck smiled at his cousin who was looking at him in the rearview mirror.

Chuck looked over at Christy who was laughing as she read a text message from Gloria. "These silly boys, thinking they can beat us. We are the smarter species, they don't stand a chance lol."

Christy replied back, "LOL so very true. I'm more concerned about us getting to the airport on time. I can't wait to get to the island so Chuck and I can finally have this first date. I know we've known each other for years but something feels different and it feels so right. It's like what took us so damn long to figure this out but at the same time I am glad we didn't because we may not have gotten through college. Or maybe we would have, who knows."

"They do say, good things come to those who wait. I don't know who "they" are but I hope for you guys it's definitely true. Steve and I are doing surprisingly good. I never thought we would end up together, he always seemed so immature but I guess that is only when he is around Chuck or all of us together. He has really surprised me and he is so sweet. Looks like we both got lucky and from the same family LMAO." Gloria had texted her back smiling like a kid on Christmas morning and she knew the smile was because of Steven.

"Gas station ahead. If anyone needs to go to the bathroom or buy anything now is the time. I do not plan on stopping til we are near the airport or if it's an emergency. That means you cuz, buy some damn diapers or something while you're in there." Steven was being serious for the most part, he did not want to make any more unnecessary stops.

"Yeah, I'll be sure to do that. Then I can throw them at you once I fill them up." Chuck was laughing as Steven pulled into the gas station.

They all piled out of the rental. While everyone was stretching Chuck immediately and quickly made his way in. He went straight to the cashier, grabbed a Pepsi and the only two four-packs of stay awake pills and handed them to the clerk. "Do you have any more of these or anything similar?"

“Sorry sir, those are the last of our inventory. Our restock order hasn’t shown up and they were due in yesterday. We have plenty of energy drinks in the coolers over there.” He pointed towards the glass door coolers.

“Yeah those things never work for me. I’ll still sleep like a baby after a redbull or a monster. Ok. I’ll take these for now and the key to the bathroom please.” Chuck paid for his items, slid the pills into his pocket just in time to see the girls and Steven walk in and made his way to the bathroom. “Sorry cuz, they’re out of the micro penis covers you were asking about.” Chuck yelled loudly as he pushed the bathroom door open.

The whole store got quiet as everyone looked over at Steven, who was too busy laughing to even reply. “Well damn, that was nicely timed and came with an audience. Ah, good times.” They all made their way to the coolers for drinks. Christy grabbed some Twizzlers for Chuck, a water and snickers for herself. Steven got a gatorade, Gloria and Harper bought cokes for themselves.

Chuck quickly opened one of the pill packs and took two pills as the instructions directed. He washed them down with a gulp of pepsi, which hurt because of the carbonation. He leaned forward to splash some water on his face, but when he stood up and looked into the mirror he did not fully recognize the reflection looking back at him. It was a slightly older and more weathered version of himself. His reflection moved as he did, he tilted his head and the reflection did as well, he raised his hand and the reflection did the same. It wasn't until they both placed their hands palm to palm on the mirror did Chuck get a flash of who he was looking at. It was Charles reflecting back at him. Chuck got a flash of memories, including the time with Jacob and Samuel, Charles meeting some unknown woman and Charles on some kind of ship. Apparently Charles's family owned a ship that he used to get to the island. Chuck's head started to feel fuzzy and dizzy, then he fell to the floor.

Steven rushed into the restroom when he heard the sound of Chuck hitting the floor. As he barged in the restroom, he could have sworn that Chuck's reflection was watching him for a moment before it disappeared out of sight. It was like the reflection forgot what was happening then snapped back to reality. Steven didn't have time to worry about that, he grabbed Chuck and shook him as he yelled his name.

Chuck came to right away, he was only down for a few seconds but it was long enough to scare his cousin and get a glimpse of Cassandra smiling at him. He shot up and tried getting to his feet but was a bit unsteady. He noticed some water on the floor and blamed the puddle for his fall.

"They seriously need to clean these bathrooms better. I went to walk towards the door and slipped in that damn puddle. Where is the manager? This is such bullshit!" Chuck stormed out of the bathroom, almost forgetting Steven, and went straight to the cashier to demand to speak to the manager.

A woman in her mid thirties was already making her way to the front when she heard all the commotion. "Excuse me sir, did I hear correctly that you slipped and fell in the restroom?"

Chuck was surprised that the woman was so quick to respond. "Yeah I did. There's a puddle right by the sink and when I went to leave the restroom, I slipped in it. Damn near broke my neck when I fell." He knew he was exaggerating but he was still getting over the shock of what he had just seen.

The manager quickly replied, “I am so sorry. Please let me refund whatever purchases you made and I will have our corporate team reach out to you to ensure you have no injuries or are in further distress.”

“Thank you. I appreciate that and your concern. There's no need to refund anything, I only purchased a drink.” He didn't need Steven and the others knowing he bought and was taking the stay awake pills. He gave the manager his contact information and began heading towards the door. “Thank you again ma'am.”

Steven had already made his way to the car but he couldn't seem to shake the thought that he saw Chuck's reflection watching them for a moment. His face showed confusion and a hint of fear, could he have actually seen what he thought he saw? Is that even possible?

Chuck was quick to notice the look of distress on his cousin's face. “Hey, you ok? You look like you saw a ghost or something.”

“How about the or something part. I must be losing my mind because I thought I saw your reflection watching you fall and me rush into the bathroom before it disappeared or synced up with you. Believe me, I know that sounds absolutely insane. Like nuthouse insane." Steven was freaking out and had no idea what he had seen.

"Maybe everything just happened so fast and your eyes were playing tricks on you? Like you were so focused on the fact that I had fallen that your brain slowed everything else down. Kinda like when someone has deja vu, it's just their brains playing tricks on them." He was trying to find a way to rationalize away Stevens fear so he wouldn't continue questioning what he saw, even if what he saw was really there. He could barely believe that he was looking at his past self, so for Steven to see it as well, only proved that what was happening wasn't confined to his mind. Which to him was a relief but also made everything a hundred times more frightening. So, he needed to make sure that those closest to him knew nothing of the horrors he lived through and the ones that may lay ahead of them.

"Yeah maybe, I was pretty scared that you may have been hurt or something was wrong. Plus, that's not even possible, it's like stuff from horror movies and we all know that shit is fake." Steven felt better and his cousin played a big part in that. "Thanks for that cuz, I thought I was losing my shit for a bit there".

“Hey, I come in handy on occasion. How about we don’t mention this to the girls, we don’t wanna freak them out or give them any reason to want to cancel the trip. I know I’ve already added enough crazy for the both of us, if we tell them about what you thought you saw then they'll drop us both off at the funny farm. We’ll be in straight jackets hugging ourselves while they’re hugging cold drinks and some island native.” Chuck was being funny and serious, plus he knew time wasn’t exactly on his side. The pills wouldn’t be working for much longer and Cassandra would be making her return to his nightmares very soon.

“I agree a million percent, no way some pool boy is gonna be anywhere near our girls. Ain’t no way in hell am I letting that happen. Nope. Nope. Nope.” Steven was fully on board with what Chuck was saying.

“Good. Here they come. Let me do the talking and I’ll make sure we make it to island fun and cold drinks.” Chuck had Steven fully convinced and knew that the mirror incident would not be a problem.

Steven nodded to Chuck and climbed into the driver's seat.

"What the hell was all that? I heard something about Chuck falling in the bathroom, then some lady manager coming out to help and then you guys left. We took advantage of her offer and got some free supplies. Plus, twenty in gas, so let's top off and head out. But while we are gassing up, someone has some explaining to do." Harper was the one to speak up to the boys while Christy and Gloria stood there just smiling.

Chuck stepped up. He took out the nozzle, started pumping the gas and explained what happened, from the "slip" in the puddle to the manager coming out to talk to them. Everything flowed together perfectly and he made sure that left no room for any crazy questions. He added that Steven was gonna drive just in case he hit his head harder than he noticed. He put the gas nozzle back, locked the cap and gave Steven the thumbs up.

Steven started the car, rolled down the window, he padded the door and yelled, "Lets move out you slow ass MFers!"

Everyone got in, bucked up and Steven pulled out of the gas station. Steven gave the rental a little more acceleration than necessary, the tires squealed and the back end fishtailed a bit. Steven let out a sinister laugh as the rental straightened out. Everyone yelled out for him to slow down and watch what he was doing.

"Oh, come on, just having a little fun, besides it wasn't that bad." Steven was still smiling from his little stunt.

Gloria punched Steven on the arm and said, "You better not do that shit again, this a rental not your own personal vehicle. You know these damn rental companies like to nickel and dime their customers for every bug and ding they can find. So, chill on the crazy antics, doofus."

"Geez, alright. Party pooper." Steven was a little bummed but he understood what she was getting at.

Chuck was smiling in the back while he was sitting with Christy. He knew Steven liked to show off and he knew why he did it this time. He was making sure none of the girls were still thinking about the gas station incident, instead they were more focused on Stevens driving and the condition of the rental. They both wanted to make sure they made their island getaway and have some much needed time with their girls. Chuck had hoped that Christy would be the only girl he would be seeing on that island, but he knew that Cassandra was already lurking around his mind.

Whose to say she wasn't waiting there for him, that the moment he set foot on the island she will have won. She would have him within her reach, in her grasp and would he be able to fight her?

Chuck looked out the window, watching the cars and trees go by, as they made their way down the expressway. He stared at his reflection waiting for it to change into something or someone else. The version of himself that he saw in the bathroom at the gas station was a slightly older and weathered version. Their ages appeared to be similar but the look in his eyes told a story of pain, loss and tragedy. A story of love that was turned into a nightmare and a hard fought battle. Chuck just wished Steven hadn't walked into the bathroom when he did. Chuck had so many questions that he wanted to ask, but the reflection never spoke to him like Cassandra did, so who knew if he would have as well.

While sitting there he noticed that his eyelids were getting heavy and the exhaustion was starting to set in. Perhaps the pills had finally stopped working and the inevitable sleep was drifting closer. It was only a matter of time before the unseen nightmare, that was Cassandra, would make her horrific return.

He felt his head getting heavier and he strained to keep his eyes open. He felt his breathing and heart rate slow down a bit. His body became relaxed and the tension just seemed to flow away, like a leaf on the wind. He felt as if everything around him was slowing down, even turning his head to look at Christy who was asleep on his shoulder, it was like watching the world in slow motion. He used the last of his strength to lay his head against Christy's and his eyes closed.

He opened his eyes and he was back standing in the house that he lived in with Cassandra. He recognized their old room, even with the only light coming from the moon. He got up, headed to the door and opened it. He made his way to the room that was his old study, he noticed that there was a glow coming from under the door. The glow was from a lit lantern that was sitting on a table in the corner of the room. As he walked into the study he saw someone sitting in the chair next to the table with the lantern.

The person's face was hidden by the darkness of the room, Chuck approached the person. The light seemed to slowly reveal the face of the person sitting in the chair and Chuck recognized him. It was the same person he saw in the mirror of the bathroom at the gas station. It was Charles and he looked as if he had been waiting for Chuck to show up.

Charles spoke first. “Evenin. I'm not sure how this is happening or how it's even possible. The last thing I remember was the day I died. My body and my mind just couldn't take any more, that day I sat here and drank the last glass of my favorite whiskey. I finished it, closed my eyes and drew my last breath. So, to be sitting here in my home with someone who bears an uncanny resemblance to myself is quite confusing, I’m sure you would agree.” Charles just looked up at Chuck from the chair.

“Confusing would have been a good word to use if this wasn’t the first time this has happened. I saw you in the mirror earlier, at least I figured it was you since I have also been getting your memories. Up until now, it has been a constant nightmare with Cassandra haunting me. I think somehow we are related or connected, maybe I am you reincarnated.” Chuck saw the look of terror come across Charles’s face when he mentioned Cassandra's name.

“N…No, it is not possible. I killed her, I made sure that there was no way she could have survived. Oh, dear God, what did I miss? I thought I had covered every possibility. I am so sorry, I had hoped and prayed that the world was free of her terror." Charles sat in his chair with tears rolling down his face. "Did she say how she survived, what happened, or what she even wants? This is some of the worst news I have gotten in a very long long time. As far as us being connected, we seem to be mirror images of each other and the fact that somehow you are gaining my memories makes it likely that in some way we are one and the same. What has me baffled is how is it possible?"

"She wants the same thing now that she wanted when you were alive. She wants us, she wants me! It's kinda terrifying, I have been trying to not sleep so I can avoid her and not die. She is horrifically powerful and I am afraid that one of these times that I fall asleep will be my last. For all we know, she's watching us and is waiting to get her revenge on one or both of us." There was a deathly silence from both men, they looked around expecting Cassandra to appear and attack them.

"Well, that was a bit awkward." Chuck spoke first. "I kinda thought she was just going to manifest out of thin air and attack. I suggest we use what time we have to figure out what you missed back then and what I can do to permanently end her. I'd rather not die any time soon, especially since I've finally started a relationship with someone I truly love."

"Congratulations. I hope you have better luck than I did." Charles smiled half-heartedly. "I spent quite a bit of time planning and researching how to end Cassandra and her terror. I had help from some friends and we tested methods and ways to get our job done."

"You are talking about Jacob and Samuel, right?" Chuck surprised him with his question.

"Wow, you really are gaining my memories and yes that is who I am referring to. It is quite remarkable that you are acquiring my memories." Charles wasn't sure how to feel about Chuck knowing what he knew. "Are you aware of the methods we planned on using to destroy her? If so, perhaps it's best not to speak of them. Especially since you say that she is haunting your dreams." Charles wasn't sure how Cassandra was able to invade Chuck's mind but it was best not to take any chances with important information.

"Yes I am and I agree the less we say the better, at least in certain regards. A close friend is assisting me with some preparations and research." Chuck smiled and winked at Charles, whose eyes widened. "I am finding out some very interesting information from the internet. Do you know what that is?"

"The inter-who? The memory sharing seems to be a one-way path. Maybe since I passed long ago, I am unable to see what you have seen." Charles was confused and curious about what has happened since his passing.

"What if we shake hands, I know this is going to sound weird, but just hear me out. What if we are the same person just at different times, so in theory, if we make contact we can pass each other information without speaking. It's worth a shot, worst case scenario nothing happens. But if it works we will know what the other does and use it to our benefit. What do you think?" Chuck was trying to think "outside of the box", he wasn't sure if it would work.

"Indeed, an interesting theory. I am willing to give it a shot, like you said in the worst case scenario nothing happens." There was one bit of information that he planned on holding back from his counterpart, he just hoped his mind was strong enough to keep it hidden. Something far more important than Cassandra and their crusade to end her.

Both men stood up, faced each other and shook hands. At first nothing happened, they just stood there, the two men were about to give up and let go. Then they each saw a flash of light and a surge of images invading their minds. Charles saw Chuck's entire life, from birth to recent events. He saw his childhood, Christy, Chuck's interactions with Cassandra, his meeting Jacob and the email that hinted at the possibility that Chloe was still alive. Chuck saw similar visions from Charles, he saw Cassandra's massacre along with Edwards murder, he saw Chloe and her death, the vivid scene of Jacob after he was mauled by Cassandra. Chuck saw the research done with Jacob and Samuel and when he was about to see the events where Charles battled Cassandra both men hit the floor.

Gasping for air, they both sat up and just looked at each other. "What happened? It was like something stopped the connection before your battle with Cassandra." Chuck was breathing so hard and fast that he began to get dizzy.

Charles grabbed Chuck to help him off of the floor, he moved him to the chair and sat him down. "I believe it was you that severed the connection. Perhaps it was too much all at once and your mind fought back." Charles knew he, in part, was also to blame for disconnection. He could feel Chuck's emotions rising quickly and the turmoil he felt was overwhelming. Plus, after seeing what Chuck learned about Chloe, he had to stop him from seeing anymore.

"That was quite intense and educational. Technology has certainly come a long way since I was alive. I see what you found out about Cassandra and your email. I suggest you let that email go, Chloe died a long time ago and it was the hardest thing I've ever had to endure. Countless nights I spent wishing I could have saved her but her mother was a poison that took her from me." As the tears were building up in his eyes Chuck could feel his pain as if it was his own.

"I am so sorry. As much as I want to say I can't imagine your pain, due to our connection, I feel your heartbreak. I can feel the hurt and anger you felt for both Chloe and for Jacob's death. How is this possible, that even though we've lived centuries apart, it is like we have lived these horrors together. I've never heard of anything like this, not even in the movies." Chuck's anger was building up and now more than ever he felt hate for Cassandra that dwelled in Charles all those years ago.

"It must be something that Cassandra has done to us. It appears we have both tasted her blood and power, though you seemed to like it more than I did. You mustn't give in to her. No matter what she offers or how persistent she becomes, you must never become like her. That is her goal. She's lonely and desperate but the connection that she and I shared now lives in you." The seriousness in his voice and the pain in his eyes was pleading with Chuck.

"I have no intention of becoming anything like her. She is a monster, raised from the deepest depths of hell and from my darkest nightmares. I will do whatever it takes to protect the ones I love and even if it means my life, I will finish what you started all those years ago. I think that hiding from her in my dreams by keeping myself awake is only making me weaker. Maybe I should make her think that I am intrigued and interested in her offer, if only to get closer to her. That way when the time comes, it will be easier to get to her and end her." Chuck was finally beginning to think clearly, but what he was proposing was incredibly dangerous.

"That is a dangerous game to play, one that I played and lost. Perhaps, with my knowledge and yours, you can do what I failed to do. Use the help you have been offered and given and I pray that you will be successful." Charles was starting to feel weak, he looked down at his hands and he noticed that they were starting to become transparent.

Chuck looked at Charles's hand and saw what he was staring at. "What's happening?"

"I think this will be the only time we will speak. I have passed all I can to you, it is up to you now. I'm feeling weaker than when we first arrived here. This was my home and the place where I was finally able to rest." Charles staggered to his dresser and poured himself and Chuck a glass of whiskey. He slid the second glass over to Chuck.

"No. Wait. I still don't know where you fought her and what happened. Please, you must stay and tell me more." Chuck pleaded with Charles.

"I'm sorry. There is nothing more I can share, I don't have the strength. But what I can tell you is that island, the one you all are going to. That was to be her final resting place. She is pulling you there. Be strong and pray. The lord will keep you safe. Now join me in a drink before I go." Charles picked up his glass, his hands were shaky.

Chuck grabbed the glass of whiskey and clinked the glass against Charles's. Both men, in unison said, "To those we love, to those we have lost and to the strength we need to protect them." They drank their whiskey and Charles vanished once he set the glass down.

Chuck sat in the chair where Charles had been sitting. His sense of purpose was renewed and he felt determination that was stronger than ever. He took a breath, savored the taste of the whiskey and he made his way downstairs. He reached for the door to leave the house, stepped outside and closed the door. He blinked and when he opened his eyes he was sitting next to Christy. She was still sleeping on his shoulder, he kissed her head.

He knew that what was next would be the most difficult and the most perilous game he had ever played. He knew he had to beat Cassandra and no matter what the cost, he would win. He would do what Charles gave his life for and he would have justice for those stolen by that monster.

Chuck took the last of the stay awake pills he had left into his hand, he rolled down the window and dropped them outside of the moving car. Chuck closed his eyes and laid his head against Christy's. He took a breath and felt himself drift off to sleep. When he opened his eyes he was standing on the same beach as before. He began walking, enjoying the mist in the air as it kissed his face. He felt his feet dig into the sand with each step until he reached logs where the bon fire was roaring. He sat down and waited.

He heard Cassandra's voice as she approached him, “Hello my beloved.”

Chapter Seven

Chuck looked over at Cassandra as she made her way closer to him. She sat down across from him and just stared into the fire. She looked over at the waves as they crashed into the shore, the mist from the waves filled the air around them. She turned her attention back to Chuck and smiled at him.

"I just love this view. I love watching the waves crash into the shore, the cool mist that fills the air and the smell of the ocean. I used to hate all of that, just the sound of the water would bring out my anger." Cassandra asked him.

"Why would such a beautiful and amazing sight cause you so much anger?" Chuck wanted to get her talking so that he could get as much information from her as possible.

"This place was my prison. I was brought here long ago, against my will, and left to die by someone who was supposed to love and protect me. I was betrayed and my heart was broken, shattered and stomped on. People hide their true colors and intentions until it is too late to do anything about it. How would you feel if the person you loved the most in this world turned out to be a wolf in sheep's clothing?" Cassandra spoke as if she was completely innocent and not deserving of such cruel treatment.

"I think I would be angry and sad, but I don't know what I would do. I suppose I would want revenge or some kind of retribution. I would want that person to feel the hurt that I am feeling. But I honestly don't know if I would act on those feelings. I would find a way to better myself and find someone who truly appreciates me, but that's probably easier said than done. It is easier to cause pain than it is to heal and move on." Chuck was being honest with her in hopes to build some kind of rapport. Part of him felt sorry for her but deep down he knew that she was only giving him bits and pieces of the true story. He knew that she had attacked Jacob and tried to kill him. She attacked Charles in their own home and she was the reason Chloe had died so young.

"It is hard to know what one would do unless they were in that situation. I have been here for so long, trapped in this paradise prison and all because I chose to let my passion turn to anger and I've learned that regret is a powerful motivator." Cassandra watched Chuck as she spoke, he looked empathetic to the hurt and pain that she was expressing.

With every bone in his body screaming not to and Charles words ringing in his mind, he got up and sat down next to her. He knew the game he was about to play was a deadly one and with one swift move she could end him but he believed he could win. Was it arrogance or desperation, he wasn't sure but in his heart he knew that she had to be stopped. He did not believe for one second she was innocent and had no blame in the events that led to her entrapment.

"May I ask you something?" Chuck asked nervously.

"Yes, of course you can my love." She responded.

"Do you know where you were taken and imprisoned?" Deep down he already knew the answer but he had to know for sure.

"All I know is that it is an island south of Florida. I know we had to have arrived by ship because well it's an island and no other way to get here. I must have been drugged with some type of sleep inducing chemicals and brought here." She could see a look of shock and surprise in his eyes. "You know what island I am on, don't you?"

"I don't think this is a coincidence because my friends and I are traveling to an island for a vacation and it seems that it may be the one you are trapped on." There was a moment while he was talking that his voice cracked. He hoped she hadn't heard it but the look she was giving him said otherwise.

"Are you nervous? Your voice cracked, so either you're nervous or hiding something." Cassandra looked at Chuck intensely as she asked him about his voice crack.

He knew he had to come up with an answer quickly. "Just a bit nervous, usually by this time you are chasing me down or threatening me." The answer was a bit accusatory but he had to draw attention away from the voice crack.

"Well, that seems a tad harsh but I suppose it's fair. I am trying to be civil and I am hoping that the sample of my power I gave you would be enough to sway you to see things my way." Her soft expression turned to a serious one.

“I am guessing that you are used to getting your way, after all you are truly a powerful woman. I never knew that something happening in your dreams could affect you in the real world. How were you able to do that?” Chuck wanted to understand her powers and how she was to develop them to be so strong. If he was able to get an understanding of it all, perhaps he could pass that knowledge to Jacob the next time they met.

“You are correct. I am very powerful and I am quite accustomed to getting my way. The two go hand in hand but at times to be truly persuasive, one must use fear as a motivational tactic. Fear can bend the strongest man to your will, it makes whole cities follow a general into war and even give the shyest man the courage to speak to the woman of his dreams. It can also cause the smartest man to make a simple mistake due to his own fears, one's plans can fall apart and come crumbling down all because of the power that fear is given. As far as my powers are concerned, just know this, it has taken centuries of practice, commitment and sacrifice to learn how to harness and increase them.” She purposely left the answer about her powers vague but went into detail about being powerful. It's a trick that's given her an advantage over others in the past.

"Intimidation? Is that really your strongest tactic?" Chuck snickered. "No offence but I've been bullied most of my childhood, so trying to scare me with words, well it's not gonna help you much."

She was stunned by his words, not since Charles has anyone been so blatantly defiant. "You remind me of someone I used to know, he outright told me that regardless of what I am, he did not fear me. He once meant the world to me, enough that I offered him immortality and a love to last a lifetime, but he is dead and gone now. Your words and your tone, they sound remarkably familiar." She could hear Charles in his voice and the anger inside her began to rise. "Don't make the same fatal mistakes that you… I mean that he once did." She knew she had almost slipped and spoke of his counterpart.

Chuck was well aware of Charles declining her offer and he knew he had struck a nerve with her. "I apologize if I offended you, it wasn't my intention. I simply meant to make you aware that I do not submit easily. I've learned that people with more power than me often think that I am pushover and lack the resolve to defend myself. Believe me, that is far from the truth." He was refusing to back down from her.

"Usually when someone says no offence or that wasn't their intention, it was truly their intention. Since you felt the need to explain yourself, I will overlook the disrespect and tone that you are giving off. Understand this, we may be in a dream that seems calm and relaxing but in an instant I can change this wonderful dreamscape into a true land of endless horror. All it would take is a simple snap of my fingers and every dark horrific nightmare you've ever had will swarm your mind, leaving you crying, sobbing vegetable." Her anger was building more and more with every ounce of resistance he gave her.

"I think we are done here." Chuck got up and began walking away from Cassandra. He looked back to see her stand up and move clear of the logs they had been sitting on. "What are you doing?" He asked suspiciously.

"You dare turn your back on me? Perhaps you are more like Charles than I realized." She glared at him. The look of anger on her face was accompanied by her fangs slowly creeping down. She felt her heart beat increasing and she wanted to lunge at him and tear at his throat.

Chuck stood there staring at her, her fangs and the look of absolute hatred in her eyes. He knew it was time to switch his game plan to defense. "How am I like him? Is it because I refuse to be intimidated? I'm sorry if that upsets you but I don't understand how standing up for myself is a bad thing. I told you that for so long I was unable to do so, now that I've learned how to, I refuse to stop. I won't be weak, not for a single moment."

She was taken back by his words. They rang all too familiar in her ears and hit her like a ton of bricks. "Your words, they are how I once felt. It was long ago but I understand them." She took a breath and calmed herself. "You're right. It is not wrong to stand up for yourself and if what you say is true, then you may not be as similar to him as I thought." She turned around and looked out at the ocean. She sighed but when she turned around he was gone. She smiled.

Chuck jolted up as the car swerved. He could hear Gloria yelling at Steven to watch where he was going.

"You know if you run over that road gator you can blow a tire." Gloria yelled at him.

"Road gator? What the hell are you talking about? It was part of a semitrucks tire." Steven snapped back.

"That's called a road gator dork. How are you a guy and you don't even know that?" Gloria teased him.

"How does that even make sense? Road gator? You're making that up, aren't you?" Steven was confused and annoyed because Gloria was snapping at him.

"She's right cuz. My dad always called it that, plus you can Google it." Chuck called up from the back seat.

"Ha! See, even Chuck knows that." Gloria was taunting Steven.

"Thanks a lot cuz. So much for having my back." Steven rolled his eyes at his cousin.

"My bad." Chuck snickered from the back seat.

Christy was still sleeping on Chuck's shoulder and started to wake up. She yawned, stretched and leaned over and kissed Chuck. "Hey there handsome."

"Hey gorgeous, did you get some good sleep?" Chuck asked while smiling back at her.

"Surprisingly I did. You are a very comfy pillow. Did you have a good nap? Woke up to you snoring and I fell back asleep." She asked.

"I did. No crazy nightmares this time, which was nice." He purposely left out the part about Cassandra making an appearance and their conversation. He also hid the fact that he met his past self and how he acquired a whole bunch of new memories.

“Well, that's a good sign, maybe this whole nightmare woman craziness is behind us now. That would be really good, then we can enjoy our vacation without any worries.” Christy was truly hopeful that Cassandra wasn't haunting him anymore and that maybe it was just from an overactive imagination.

“That would be great, to be able to enjoy ourselves without her creeping around my head and terrifying my dreams. I guess we will just have to wait and see.” He let her hold on to her hopes of a carefree and enjoyable trip, but he knew better. He wouldn't be free of her, not until she was permanently dead and gone. He still wasn't sure how she had survived the confrontation with Charles and he knew Jacob said he didn't know much about what happened on the island.

She smiled, stretched again letting out a loud moan and yelled. “Oh, this is gonna be a great vacation. It's going to be epic and definitely unforgettable.”

Harper yelled back, "Hell yeah. I'm gonna get drunk and make some fun and probably fuzzy memories."

"That is if our driver here can get us to the airport in one piece." Gloria was still teasing Steven, even though she could see it was annoying him.

"Do you wanna drive? Because I can pull over and let you drive, you know since I'm such a terrible driver and all." Steven was making sure she knew he was getting tired of the teasing.

"Oh relax, I'm just messing with you. You're doing a great job driving and getting us there." She leaned over and kissed Steven on the cheek and tapped his nose.

"Uh huh, sure." Steven smirked and gave her a playful side eye look.

Chuck grabbed his phone and noticed that he had a couple of text message notifications on his screen.

The first one was from his mom, in their family group chat. "Hey sweetie, hope you kids are having fun and being safe. Let us know when you get to the airport. Love you."

Chuck replied back, "I will. Love you too."

The second message was from Jacob. "Hope everything is going smoothly. Message me back when you get this. I need to ask you about something."

Chuck was wondering what Jacob needed to ask him about. He knew there was a lot of stuff he had to update Jacob on, especially the visit from Charles. He would message him back and see what was going on, especially since Christy was busy on her phone.

"Hey Jacob. Just seen your text, hope everything is OK. What did you need to ask me about? I have some info to update you on and you're not gonna believe what I have to tell you."

Chuck sent the text and waited for Jacobs' reply, which only took a few minutes.

Jacobs text read. "Hey. I'm doing OK. I wanted to ask you about that email you got from the website inquiry. Did the respondent leave a name or anything? I have reason to believe it may be a site run by humans and vampires."

Chuck replied. "Yeah, the name they gave was CJ. There was no last name or anything else. Do you think you know who it is? Why do you think the site is run by both humans and vampires?"

As Jacob read Chuck's reply, he was shocked by the initials that the respondent left. It was either a coincidence or it was someone he knew very well that had disappeared many years ago. “There is a chance that I know this person but I need to look into it before I can confirm it. What is the info you have to tell me about? The info that I won't believe lol.”

Chuck wasn't happy that Jacob wasn't telling him who he thought responded to him. “Please do keep me updated on who the respondent might be. My info, I hope you're sitting down for this one, I had a visit from Charles in one of my dreams.”

Jacob was, yet again, shocked by what he just read. “What? How? He died many years ago, I found his body and I burned it. I buried his ashes with his family near Chloe's grave.”

Chuck texts him back. “I don't know how, there must be some sort of connection between him, Cassandra and me. Trust me, it's as weird and confusing for me as it is for you. He looked just like me except he looked older, more worn down. We talked about a possible connection that links me to the past and then with a hand shake we exchanged memories. It was like for a moment we were literally one person with memories flowing between our minds. He knows that you are alive and helping me but I think he cut the connection before I was able to see what happened between him and Cassandra in his final days. It was intense and left me with a lot of questions."

"He left me behind when he and Samuel left with Cassandra. We had found a way to drug her and keep her unconscious while they took her to the island. He never told me where it was or what transpired. I just know that he came back alone and he came back to die in his own home." Replied Jacob.

"Island? What island? Did he say anything to you about where this island was?" Chuck was getting really nervous now that he knew Cassandra was for sure taken to some unknown island and he and his friends were heading to a strange island for vacation.

"There was no name for the island back then. I just know it was south of what is now Florida. Back then the plan was to travel by ship to this island that his parents frequented and end her there. I was supposed to go with them but Charles drugged me and left me behind. I think it was his way of protecting me since he wasn't able to when she attacked me. Samuel never made it back and neither did a woman named Erica. She became part of our plan when she attempted to be Cassandra's spy. She double crossed Cassandra, by helping us when originally she had planned to give away our position and plans. Maybe she turned on them while on the island. At this point, I have many questions like you do. Are you able to speak with him again?" Jacob asked.

"Unfortunately, no. He said his final goodbye after a glass of whiskey and he disappeared. I think he used whatever energy he had to show me what he did and he left. I wish I would have been able to ask him more or be able to recall more memories but at the moment, that's all I have." Chuck sent that text and then added more. "I think the island where he took Cassandra is the one my friends and I are headed to. The way I found this island is making me think she's more than just a figment haunting my dreams. I think she is physically and mentally luring me back there."

"I've only heard of a few stories where a vampire was able to cheat death, but without knowing how Charles supposedly killed her, I don't know what we can do. I can tell you the methods we prepared and what we used to sedate her but clearly something didn't work or go as planned. Have you seen her recently?" He replied back.

"Yes. After my visit from Charles, I decided that I needed to see how much info I could get from her without making her suspicious. I had fallen back asleep and there she was. We spoke for a bit, she tried to intimidate me and I told her that I don't scare easily. She then told me she believed that she was on an island that she referred to as her prison paradise. She gave the same location that you did and she believed that she had been drugged. She spoke a lot about betrayal and heartbreak. I think she's trying to win me over with a sad sob story."

"She will try anything and everything to get you on her side and make you become like her. There are no limits to her madness and no end to her horrific intentions. We must stay strong and vigilant. You NEED to be careful when you speak with her, she has a way of getting information out of a person. Most importantly, you can not let her drink a single drop of your blood. It is imperative that you avoid that. I believe that was Charles's downfall, she was able to take his blood and found out about our plans. This sped up our time frame and changed things significantly." Jacob was beginning to feel anxious about the situation and you could tell by his message.

"OK. I know I need to be cautious with her and how I interact with her. I will see if I can get any more info without getting myself killed or turned into a vampire. I'll keep you updated on anything new and you let me know about the website stuff. I'll message you soon. Be safe." Chuck needed a break from the conversation with Jacob. He knew Jacob was holding back something about the respondent from the website but he didn't understand why he wouldn't tell him.

"OK my friend. You be safe as well. I'll let you know if I find out anything about her. Talk to you soon." The moment that Jacob hit send he sighed knowing that things were only going to get more complicated and much more dangerous from here on out.

Chuck put his phone away and looked out the window. He could see a storm was starting to move into the area. It seemed fitting considering the storm that they were all heading to on that island. He wanted so badly to tell his friends that they needed to turn the car around and just go home. He thought about faking being sick just to convince them or even purposely getting hurt so that they would spend the next week visiting him in the hospital. Anything would be better than the uncertainty that laid ahead of them. What he hated more than anything was that the people he cared about the most would be put in dangerous situations. The worst part is that they wouldn't even believe him if he tried to warn them. They would check him into a psych hospital, padded walls and all.

He would just have to hope that Jacob would be enough back up and they would never know the truth. He would have to find a reason or a way to sneak off and pray that he made it back to them. There was a very good chance that Christy would believe him but the others would just laugh at him. He looked down at his hands, balled up his fists and prayed. He prayed for the strength to battle the evil waiting for him and for the safety of his loved ones. Even if it meant his life, as long as they made it home, he would accept that fate.

Christy glimpsed over at Chuck and could tell that he was struggling with something. The look of distress is his eyes, the frown on his lips and the tension building up in his shoulders. She could feel how stiff and rigid his posture was becoming and it worried her. She knew that he was hiding something and it terrified her that it had something to do with Cassandra. She contemplated asking him about what was on his mind but she wasn't sure if he would tell her. She looked down at her phone and decided to text him, she figured he may text it instead of saying it. "Hey. Are you ok? I've known you long enough to know when something is going on in that brain of yours."

Chuck looked down at his phone and smiled. "Yeah, I'm ok. Just got a few things on my mind. You doin ok?" He tried to keep the messaging casual.

"I'm good but I am worried about you. I know this stuff with Cassandra is weighing on you but don't forget, I am here with you. Whatever you need, just let me know. And don't give me that BS line that nothing is going on or happening. I've seen marks appear on your neck and reactions you've had in your sleep. I've seen you look afraid and I have never seen the look of fear on your face like that in the entire time I've known you. So please don't tell me it's nothing or you're fine." She could see him reading most of the text as she typed it.

Chuck replied. "You're right, I'm not fine or ok. I am terrified. I'm worried something bad is going to happen to one of you guys and I won't be able to forgive myself for it. There is so much happening that I don't even know how to explain it all. It honestly sounds like a horror movie, but I couldn't make this shit up if I tried. If i could though lol i'd be rich."

"It's up to you, what you want to tell me, whether it's all of it or parts you feel are more important. Or even bits and pieces. Whatever it is, no matter how far fetched it sounds, I won't make fun of you or laugh. Even if it means I have to whoop some supernatural vampire ass, I got your back babe. I've seen how Sam and Dean do it, we got this shit." She tried to lighten up the mood a bit, even though she was serious. She would fight whomever and whatever for him.

To add to the moment of humor, Chuck started playing the theme song of the Supernatural TV show, "Carry on My Wayward Son" By Kansas. They both started laughing.

He texted her. "Thank you. It really means a lot to me to know that you have my back and that I'm not alone in this. If you really want to know the truth of the situation, I will tell you but I can guarantee that it is going to scare you. I honestly don't know how this situation is going to go but I do have a bad feeling that it is not going to end well."

Christy replied. “I want to know all of it, scary or not, and we have plenty of time to go over it. So, when you're ready to start just let me know. I figure that the pic that looked like you at the restaurant was an extremely old one of you and her. Way too much of a convenience to be anything else. And the night you disappeared I knew you must have gone somewhere familiar, my guess was the big house we passed.”

Chuck was impressed by how much she was actually paying attention. “Spot on so far. Yes I did go to my old house and I had some memories come back to me that night. And a lot more memories have popped up since then.” He wasn't quite ready to reveal Jacob to her, mainly because he didn't wanna freak her out. He told her about the website he found and the response from the site administrator.

“Wow!! A lot more has happened than I realized. Is there more? How about the weird incident at the gas station?” Christy was shocked by all that he had been hiding, but also relieved that he was willing to share the details with her.

“The gas station. Yeah, that was an interesting one. I saw me, well the old me, in the reflection in the mirror.

Then when I fell asleep in here next to you, I spoke to him." He gave her most of the details about the chat he had with Charles and the memory swap that occurred.

"So, if you, or the old you, attempted to destroy her what went wrong? And where did he take her?" She was really getting into the events that happened.

"Don't freak out but I think the island that we are going to, is the place where it all went down. He didn't give me all the details before he vanished but I believe we are headed to her resting place. I don't think it's a coincidence either, the way I found the island was very strange and I think she's behind it." Chuck watched her face as she read the message he had just sent. He could see the fear rise a bit in her eyes.

She replied. "So, we are going to an island that is home to a vampire that you were once married to, in another life. You don't know how the plan failed but you have ideas on what can be used to kill her based on memories you gained from him. All this and we have no back up or help from anyone?" She wanted to make sure she had the basics covered.

Now Chuck felt it may be necessary to bring up Jacob but he'd only give her some of the details. “Yes and no. Yes to all that but we do have some back up. I, we, have a friend that I used to know from a long long time ago. He asked me to keep his presence to myself, for his safety and ours but I know you're going to ask. Yes, he is a vampire. These are some of the strangest texts we have ever shared. But he is on our side and knows more details of the weapons and things we can use to kill her.” Chuck was now getting nervous about sharing this information with Christy.

“Well, that is both terrifying and comforting. So, do you know what she wants? Is it something we can just hand over and hope she leaves us alone?” Christy could feel her heartbeat starting to get a little faster.

“There is only one thing she wants and it's the same thing she wanted all those years ago. ME. She wants the love that she lost and left her for dead.” Chuck was hesitant to hit send on that text but he did reluctantly.

“She's definitely not getting what she wants. I don't like to share, especially with a blood sucking monster bitch like her.” Now she was feeling a bit more angry than scared.

Chuck smiled, pulled her closer and kissed her. She really had no idea how much it meant to him that she was so willing to fight for him. Even against an immortal killing machine, she had no intention of giving him up. It made him happy and it gave him a strength that he never knew he had. He had already decided he would do whatever it took to make sure she and the others were safe but with Christy he wanted to make sure he survived with them. He wanted a future with her and he wanted to make all kinds of new memories with her.

He looked her in the eyes, smiled and told her that he loved her. She smiled and with watery eyes she told him the same. They sat there just holding hands and enjoying the moment. He squeezed her hand and said "I need to text you something else." She looked at him with a nervous look.

"So, it's not confirmed or anything but I have a strange feeling that Chloe may not be as dead as originally believed. The respondent from the website said some things that gave me the feeling that she may be alive somewhere. I don't think Cassandra has any idea about this and my old friend is looking into a few things for me."

Christy just looked at him after reading the text. She looked down again for a moment before responding. “So, is she kinda like your daughter or like a distant relative? This was not something I was expecting to read lol would she even recognize you or the past you? This is confusing, scary and exciting all at the same time.”

Chuck laughed. “I honestly don't know what that would make her and I. To me, she feels like my kid, which is absolutely insane. But it's still just an idea, there is no proof she is alive, so it could just be the old me hoping that she survived somehow.”

Christy replied back to him. “Gotcha. So, just in case it happens to be true, I know about it. But there's no guarantee. This is definitely not the vacation I thought we were gonna be having. We will just have to take it one step at a time and make the best of the situation and time we have for each other.”

“You are absolutely amazing. I don't know how I got so damn lucky to find someone like you but I am very thankful for you.” Chuck sent her that last text before he hugged her tight. In the back of his mind, he was hoping that Chloe was still alive and that they all made it out of this battle in one piece.

Chapter Eight

Everyone was excited that they were finally getting to the airport. They made one last stop at the gas station to gas up the rental and clean it out. They all grabbed a coffee for the wait in the airport except for Chuck, he got a large pepsi. He liked the taste of coffee but only in the morning, the caffeine had no effect on him. Plus, he knew the effect coffee had on his stomach, so he went with the ice cold pepsi. Once all the garbage was cleaned out they ran the rental through the car wash and headed to the drop offsite at the airport.

Steven parked the rental and put the keys in the drop off box. He took pictures all around the rental, he had taken pictures of the gas gauge and the mileage counter. He wasn't taking any chances with the rental company, so he emailed the company the pictures he took and sent himself a copy to his email.

“Is all that really necessary?” Harper asked Steven, with a hint of annoyance in her voice.

Steven replied. “It absolutely is necessary. I know someone who worked at a small local rental car place and the general manager would charge people for every little knick and bump they could find. The place was a rip off and run by a bunch of crooks."

"Well damn. I guess it's better to be safe than sorry." Said Harper.

They began making their way to the check in line, dropped their luggage off and made it through security. The TSA agents had Chuck and Steven step out of line to get wanded. The girls thought it was funny and were making jokes while they waited for them. Chuck looked over at the girls giving them a funny dirty look. The TSA agent looked at him disapprovingly and shook his head. Steven was nervous and anxious to get through the line. He elbowed Chuck and gave him a stern look. The TSA agent waved them through and was staring at Steven.

Once they made it pass the security checks they headed towards their boarding gate. They were informed that there was still an hour before the plane was scheduled to start letting people on the plane. They sat down in the waiting area and waited for their boarding group to be called.

Chuck pulled out his phone to text Jacob. “Hey just to update you, we are at the airport. We should be boarding soon, roughly about an hour. Christy knows about everything, except you. I told her I have some help from an old friend but she doesn't know your name. She's on board with helping us and to be honest, it is a relief to know she doesn't think I'm insane. Don't forget your flight is tonight. It's a short flight so it'll still be night time when you arrive. I'll message you when we land. Talk soon.”

He knew that with it being daytime still Jacob was probably sleeping, so he wasn't expecting a reply back. He put his phone away, leaned back in the seat and closed his eyes. Just as he was about to fall asleep, he felt something cold and wet on the side of his face. His eyes shot open to see Christy standing next to him with a twenty ounce bottle of Pepsi. She was doing her best to not laugh at the fact that she startled him with a drink.

“A little jumpy?” She asked with a smile. “I can keep the drink if you're afraid of it.” She snickered.

“Ha ha. You just got lucky and caught me off guard. I was about to doze off then I felt the cold on my skin, don’t worry I'll get you back later.” Chuck smiled at her as he grabbed the cold drink from her.

"Yeah, we'll see. But now I will be keeping an eye on you sir." Christy said with a smirk.

"Oh really? I'll keep that in mind." He looked behind her and nodded his head. She looked behind her and that gave him the opportunity to move closer and poke her sides. "BOO!!!" Chuck yelled.

Christy jumped, much higher than he did with the cold bottle. She turned around and gave him a playful, dirty look. "Well, excuse me. That was rude." She was a little embarrassed that he was able to trick her so easily.

"Told ya I would get you back." Chuck grinned with pride.

"Yeah, you did. I just didn't think it would be so soon. That was pretty good." Christy nodded her head in approval.

They sat there and joked for a bit, both taking sips of their drinks. Chuck had his pepsi and she had a nice hot coffee. Christy moved closer to Chuck and put her head on his shoulder. She told him that he was a good pillow. Just as she was about to drift off for a nap, there was an announcement over the intercoms. "Flight 225 will now begin boarding." The group made their way to the boarding line. It was a small line because the plane was smaller than huge 747's, this was a small twenty seater plane. Plus, like Chuck had told Jacob, it was a short flight. The flight was going from Jacksonville, Florida straight to the island.

As they began loading the plane, Chuck started to feel anxious. He already knew that he had a daunting task ahead of him, but as he sat in his window seat on the plane, it became terrifyingly real. Not that he doubted the severity of the situation, but once the plane landed on that island, he would have to face an evil he never dreamed was possible. What added to his fear was the uncertainty of how everything was going to play out. Would they all make it back home alive or would some or all of them die? Could Cassandra actually be killed or was he doomed to repeat the same mistakes that Charles did? His mind was racing with so many possibilities and outcomes, so many "what if" scenarios and he started to feel claustrophobic in his seat. He gripped the arms of the chair and he could feel his heart beat picking up.

Christy had sat down next to Chuck after she stored her and Chuck's carry bags in the overhead compartment. After she sat down, she noticed that Chuck's knuckles were turning white from gripping the armrest so hard. She put her hand on top of his and kissed his cheek. She noticed he had let his grip loosen just slightly, so she gently placed her hand on the side of his face that was near the window. She applied just enough pressure so that he would turn towards her, she looked into his eyes, smiled and gave him a kiss.

The moment her lips touched his, he felt the fear and tension melt away. His heart slowed its pace, his grip on the armrest loosened and he felt a bit more at ease. He looked at her and smiled.

“Not what that was for but thank you. I definitely needed that.” Said Chuck.

“I could tell. You looked like you were either gonna have a panic attack or explode. I thought that maybe a kiss might help or a shot of vodka.” She snickered trying to bring him some humor to help him relax.

Chuck laughed a little. “The moment we stepped foot on this plane, the reality of what we're about to face hit me. It scares the hell out of me.”

“We will get through this Chuck. I'm not exactly sure how but I know that together we will beat her.” She was trying to be reassuring, when in all honesty, she was terrified too.

Just then Steven plopped down in the seat in front of Chuck, followed by Gloria and Harper. The fasten your seat belts sign lit up and the plane began to start moving. Steven, Gloria and Harper began cheering as the plane lifted off. Once the plane was in the air and on its way to their destination the seat belts sign was turned off. Chuck was looking out of the window as they flew over south Florida, in the distance he could see the point where the land ran out and the ocean was all that remained. This only lasted for a short while. Soon he saw some land, he assumed it was part of the Florida Keys and shortly after that he saw their destination. La Isla de La Noche, the sight of it sent chills running up and down his spine.

At that exact moment, Chuck started to get a throbbing headache. He closed his eyes and put his head against the headrest of his seat. He instantly saw a flash of light and a wave of memories flooded his brain. He saw Charles meeting with Carolyn for the sedatives, he saw the meeting he had with John about the ship and going to see Captain James, and he saw what Charles did to keep Jacob safe from Cassandra. Chuck could tell there was some romantic tension between Charles and Carolyn, he wondered why Charles or Jacob hadn't mentioned her.

Perhaps Charles never got the chance to tell Jacob about her.

Christy could see something was happening with Chuck. He looked very disoriented and confused for the moment. She saw him put his head back, it looked like he fell asleep, once he sat forward he just seemed out of it. She was concerned about him and she placed her hand on his.

"Are you ok?" She asked him.

"What's your definition of ok?" He chuckled. "Just had a surge of memories hit me, it was a bit overwhelming this time. I swear it's like the closer we get to this damn island the stronger the memories are. It seems that Charles had a secret love interest that he got some type of sedative from to knock Cassandra out and bring her to this island. He was smart but even that wasn't enough to keep him from dying shortly after he returned home."

"Huh. What do you mean he died shortly after returning home? Was he injured or something?" Christy started wondering if Chuck was holding back more information that she realized.

"From what he had told me, not too long after getting back from his confrontation with Cassandra. He said his body was at a point where it was beyond exhaustion and it just gave out. He sat down to rest and well, it was a permanent rest. The only thing was that he never gave me any of the details of what happened on the island. It was like he withheld that so I wouldn't make the same mistakes that he did. I guess with the times being so different he had hoped that we could find a more permanent and better solution." Chuck was merely guessing at his other half's intentions.

"Why would he want to hide that? Wouldn't it be more helpful to know what he did so that way you can avoid doing the same things? That seems like a better way to avoid repeating mistakes. Do you know what kind of sedative he was able to get? I would think those would be hard to come by back then." Christy was as confused as Chuck was and probably more confused than him at the same time.

"I wish I knew Christy. All I can do now is make a plan with the information that I have and hope it'll be better than what he had when he was alive. It doesn't sound very promising but we live in very different times and we have the internet. I can't imagine Charles had access to much info on vampires like we do, whether it is fake or not, that is a big advantage for us." He wasn't one hundred percent confident with that but he knew he also had Jacobs' help.

"I believe we can come up with something that will solve this problem once and for all. Who knows, we might just find some help while we are on the island. I bet the locals probably have an urban legend that involves her, you know, like the moth man or bigfoot." She was trying to stay positive and keep a level head when all of this sounded like doom.

"That's a good point, there's no way she has gone completely unnoticed for all this time. Plus, if that's the case then I'm betting we can find a person or two who are experts in the local legend." Chuck smiled at Christy.

"Did you seriously just reference the frog brothers from "The Lost Boys" movie?" She looked at Chuck with a hint of annoyance.

His smile slowly faded. "Kinda yeah. But there just might be someone who is really familiar with her legend. I'm being serious. There is always someone who gets so obsessed with their town's history that they dig deep into it to find the basis or beginning of the legend."

"I suppose you're right, we just need to figure out how to find that person and if they're obsessed in a good or bad way. We don't want someone who is so consumed by her story that they lead us to her because they want to be turned into a vampire." She made a good point, they had much more to lose than anyone who was obsessed with Cassandra's story. If they were going to make it out of this hellish nightmare then they needed to be extremely careful.

"Well, it seems we have the beginning of our plan. Find some helpful local intel about her and go from there." Chuck was truly grateful for Christy and her help.

There was an announcement over the speakers in the plane. They were approaching the island and would be landing very soon. The fasten your seat belts sign came on and the flight attendants made their rounds to see if anyone needed any help.

Chuck thought that Steven and the girls had been asleep for most of the plane ride. He noticed Harper adjust in her seat and glimpse back at him and Christy. He wondered how much she had heard of his conversation with Christy and what she thought about it. He looked at Christy, typed into his phone that Harper had been listening and showed it to her.

Christy read the message on Chuck's phone and looked over at Harper. She saw Harper quickly turn around when Christy looked in her direction. She found it quite strange that Harper would snoop on them and then try to hide. She planned to ask her about it once they got off the plane. Christy noticed the plane was making it decent and she watched the ground come closer and closer until the bump of the wheels let them know the plane had landed.

Once the plane came to a full stop, they began retrieving their carry-on items from the overhead compartment and started lining up to exit the plane. They shuffled through the boarding hall and headed towards the baggage claims area. Harper kept glancing over at Chuck and Christy as they made their way over hand in hand. Christy noticed her awkward glances and decided to go have a chat with her.

“I'll be right back.” She said to Chuck as she let go of his hand to walk over to Harper.

Harper noticed Christy making her way towards her. “Hey you. How'd you like that flight? It was faster than I thought it would have been.” There was a hint of nervousness in her voice.

“Yeah, the flight was fine. I noticed you were eavesdropping on my convo with Chuck. I hope you don't make a big deal out of what you heard, he is just working through some strange nightmares that he had.” She was trying to downplay what they were talking about so Harper wouldn't cause a problem by telling the others.

“I guess it was one hell of a nightmare. It almost seems like you two were making plans on finding someone once we got to the island and searching for some type of urban legend creature. Sounded pretty damn weird to be honest with you.” Harper wasn't holding back her thoughts about the conversation she had overheard.

“Well yeah, when you put it that way it does sound kinda crazy. We were just working out how a movie would handle his dream if it was like a plot or something. You know Chuck watches a lot of movies, it helps him to think of the nightmare as a movie. I know it sounds bizarre but I read that it can help people with PTSD or people with recurring nightmares. I'm like his therapist with benefits.” Christy was doing her best to get Harper to buy into her story.

Harper laughed. “You really do like your fixer uppers, don't you?”

Christy was caught off guard by that comment but she played it off and laughed as well. “Chuck is different, he means a lot to me, if I can help him work through these nightmares is it really that bad? I want to help him and in the process help us. I feel like it brings us closer and more so on an intimate level.”

“Hey, whatever makes you happy Christy. Just be careful, make sure he doesn't suck you into those nightmares so deep that you lose the reason why you're helping him.” Harper was truly concerned for her friend and her mental well-being.

“I will, I promise.” Christy moved towards Harper and gave her a hug.

Harper hugged her back and smiled. “Ok. I’m glad we got that straightened out. If you need any help or anything just let me know, I am here for you guys.”

“Thank you. I appreciate that.” Said Christy with a big smile.

After they all had their luggage, they made their way to the front of the airport to catch a cab to the hotel. Chuck was able to flag down a mini-van cab, they loaded up the luggage and gave the driver the name of the hotel.

He nodded. “Yes. Yes I know this place. Beautiful place. Muy elegante. My name es Ruben.” The driver was very friendly, he had a hispanic accent, and he spoke a mixture of spanish and broken english. “Where are you from?”

Chuck answered “We are from Indiana, not too far from Chicago. How long have you lived here on the island?”

“Ah yes, Chicago. I know that place, I want to visit someday. I live here since I was a child. Long time with mama, papa y mi hermana. My sister. She leave and go to Miami for school.” Ruben beamed with pride as he spoke of his sister.

Chuck replied. “That's awesome, I hope she does really well at school. Ruben, is the hotel far from the towns? In case we want to go sight seeing and not get lost.”

“No. Not far at all. Maybe fifteen minutes from town if you walk. You call Ruben, I get you there in five. I can show you around town if you want.” They had arrived at the hotel, Ruben wrote down his phone number on a piece of paper and handed it to Chuck. “You call me, I know this island very well.”

"Thank you. We will definitely be calling you." Chuck paid Ruben for the trip and tipped him.

Everyone got their luggage out of the trunk of the taxi and made their way into the hotel. The name of the hotel was La Noche Hotel and Resorts. The front was heavily decorated with flowers and there was even a welcoming group. They placed floral lays around the group's neck and handed them complimentary drinks. They were very colorful with little umbrellas and fresh fruit on skewers sticking out of the top. The group was escorted to the front desk by the bellhop who had already loaded their luggage onto a cart and pushed it behind them.

As they approached the front desk, the manager greeted them with a smile and a warm reception. "Welcome to La Noche, we hope your stay with us is memorable and if you require anything our concierge desk is open day and night. What name is your reservation under?"

Since Chuck made all the arrangements, he was the one to speak first. "Hi and thank you. Our reservation is under Chuck Stone."

"Ah yes. I have you in Bungalow five. Our bellhop here will escort you to the bungalow and see that you have everything you need. As requested I have five room cards for you and your dinner reservation will be ready for you this evening at nine o'clock pm. I hope you have a great evening and don't forget we are here if you need anything." The manager smiled and handed the key cards to Chuck.

As they began following the bellhop, Steven nudged Chuck's arm. "Umm.... one bungalow? You do know there are five of us right?"

Chuck smiled. "Trust me cuz. You are going to be pleasantly surprised. I got a really good deal on this bungalow."

As they approached bungalow five, Steven and the girls were in awe and began cheering Chuck. The bungalow was a single cabin like structure with two levels, a wrap-around balcony and porch and a hot tub on the left side of the porch. Once they entered the bungalow, there was a unanimous "wow" from everyone. There were three bedrooms upstairs, a shared bathroom between two of the rooms and the master bedroom had its own bathroom. Downstairs had another bathroom, a living room area with a big tv, an open kitchen with a table that seated six people. On the table was an arrangement of freshly cut flowers and a bottle of champagne. The bellhop unloaded the luggage next to the sofa in the living room and waited patiently to ensure everyone was settled. Steven walked over to him, tipped him and thanked him.

"I hope this isn't too small for you guys." Chuck joked.

"Wow Chuck. This is amazing. How were you able to afford this? Don't get me wrong I am extremely grateful but holy shit this is extravagant." Gloria said as she was looking around the bungalow.

Chuck smiled. "Like I said, I got a really good deal on the reservation. But I do have some slightly upsetting news for some of you. I really hope you won't be too upset with me." Chuck paused and looked down at his feet, trying his best not to smile as he looked up at everyone. "So…. Christy and I have dibs on the master bedroom." He started laughing as everyone rolled their eyes at him.

"If that's the bad news then let's get this party started." Said Steven as he grabbed the bottle of champagne and popped it open. He poured everyone a glass and handed it to them. "A toast." They all raised their glasses. "To Chuck, for finding us this amazing destination getaway. And to all of us, may the memories we make here stay with us for a lifetime and may we always remember that we always have each other. No matter where life takes us, we always keep each other in our hearts and in our minds. Cheers!" They clinked their glasses together and drank the champagne.

The friends began to make their way to the rooms. Chuck carried his and Christy's luggage upstairs to the master bedroom. Steven carried up his luggage and came back down to bring up the girls' stuff.

Gloria walked over to Harper. "Hey sis, I hope you don't mind me staying with Steve in his room. If you need me to, I can switch off between sleeping in here with you and with him."

"Glo, I am not a little kid. I don't need you sharing a bed with me like when we were little. I will be ok, plus I may need privacy in case I meet someone while we are here." Harper smiled slyly.

"Eww, I didn't need that thought in my head." Gloria said as she playfully punched her sister on the arm. "Just be safe and put a damn sock on the door or something as a warning."

“My sock or…?” Harper started laughing as she went into her room.

Gloria rolled her eyes and chuckled at her sister. She went into the room and found Steven with a rose in hand. She went over to him, took the rose and kissed him. “Mmm, finally alone.” She gave him a deep passionate kiss, she stepped back and smiled at him. “I gotta pee. BRB.”

Steven laughed as she made her way to the bathroom. Once she closed the door he rushed over to his luggage bag, grabbed a small brown teddy bear that he had bought for her and placed it against the pillows on the bed. When she came out of the bathroom she saw the bear and ran over to it. She picked it up and hugged it, smiling from ear to ear. She hugged Steven and then ran to Harper's room to show her the bear.

Chuck and Christy laid down after they each got their suite cases situated. Christy had hung up a couple of dresses that she bought for the trip. She put her makeup and hair products in the bathroom on the counter. Chuck just put his suitcase on the chair in the room and opened one of the side pockets. He opened it just enough to see Chloe's doll, he smiled and put it away. He walked over to bed and leaned back against the pillows. Once Christy was done she had joined him. They set a timer to go off in an hour.

Christy laid her head on Chuck's chest and they both dozed off. Within minutes Chuck was already in the familiar scene, he was standing on the beach again. He looked around and decided to explore a different area this time. He passed the fire pit and log seats, he continued towards a small mountainous area. He noticed there was a cave entrance at the bottom of the mountain. As he made his way towards the cave he could tell he was being followed. He called out into the night. "You might as well come out, I know you're not far behind me Cassandra."

"Impressive. Especially for a human. I see you have finally arrived at my island. I can feel your presence, you are much closer to me than you think. Have you had time to reconsider my offer? I can give you eternity and forever to do whatever you want whenever you want." Cassandra felt a familiar impatience with Chuck that she recalled feeling with Charles.

"I think I'm going to have to pass on that. The idea of watching everyone I love die just doesn't seem like something I am interested in. But I do appreciate the offer, it was really tempting for a minute there. I do have a question for you though, what is with this cave? Something about it seems familiar to me." Chuck was trying to stall her so he could get closer to the cave and closer to the timer going off to wake him up.

"This is the cave where I was imprisoned. For years I fed off of the blood of small insignificant creatures until I was freed. This is where I buried the last pieces of my broken heart. This is where you left me to die because you didn't have the nerve to finish the job. I'm not entirely sure how Charles was able to drug me and keep me sedated for so long but when I finally woke up this cave was all I had. The damp smell, the cold air, and the loneliness of absolute silence." Cassandra was filled with such anger and despair as she spoke of the cave.

"What do you mean he couldn't finish what he started? He brought you all the way out here and didn't have the decency to make sure he completed what he set out to do? He left you to decades of isolation, which is truly inhumane." Chuck was trying to be sympathetic to her and do his best to get as much information as he could.

"Inhumane. Yes, that is an excellent word to describe what was done to me. You have quite a way with words my love, it is something your predecessor truly lacked." It was true, Cassandra enjoyed the way Chuck spoke. He was clearly much more educated than Charles and he had no problem showing his intelligence.

Chuck entered the cave and began looking around. He didn't exactly know what he was looking for but he needed to figure out where Charles failed. He had hoped he'd find something, even the tiniest clue could be helpful. As he walked deeper into the cave he noticed Cassandra had stopped following him about five feet back. "Is there something over here that upsets you?" He was compelled to ask, even if it was an obvious answer.

"Everything in this place upsets me." She answered with a hint of disgust in her voice.

Chuck had taken a step forward and slid on something that made him fall. He looked down and saw what he slipped on. It was a wooden stake. He could see that it was discolored, which to him meant it had blood on it. He picked it up and saw the fear and anger in Cassandra's eyes.

All in one moment he saw her flee the cave abruptly and the timer went off that woke him up. He sat up immediately, looked at Christy, and said "I think I know how he failed".

Chapter Nine

Jacob had made it to the airport and thanks to Chuck it was already late in the evening when boarding started. He made it through security and the baggage check with no problems. He was walking to his seat and stored his bookbag in the overhead compartment. His seat was an aisle seat away from the window. He guessed that was Chuck's way of making it easier for him to get on and off the plane. He noticed that Chuck seemed smarter and more cautious than Charles. Their differences were very interesting but the one thing that remained the same was their compassion and consideration of others. With Chuck, it was clear that Christy and his friends were very important to him and like Charles he would protect the ones he loved regardless of the cost to himself. Charles had the means to get things done mainly because of his parents' money. He was smart but comparing the two was difficult because they lived in very different eras.

As Jacob sat there he thought back to when Charles had returned from the island. He was so angry with him for leaving him behind that he almost didn’t go to see him. Charles knew how much he wanted to be a part of taking down Cassandra but as John told him, it was Charles’s way of fulfilling his father's wish of protecting Jacob. He always thought that if he had been there then maybe things would have ended differently. Maybe Charles would have been able to live a longer life, a happier life. One with Carolyn and the son he never got a chance to meet.

A son that Jacob watched over from the shadows, like Charles would have watched over him if things had been different. He wished Charles could have had the chance to be the father he had always dreamed of being. So many possible scenarios and what ifs had played through Jacobs mind over the years but the one he was living now was never one of them. Jacob finally had the chance to protect Charles, even if it was Chuck that he was watching out for. Jacob had come to see that they were one and the same person. Maybe Chuck was related to Charles, his bloodline moving through the years until the time was necessary to come back and finish what he started all those years ago.

Jacob had been so lost in thought that he didn't realize that the plane was beginning its descent onto the island. There was a heaviness in the pit of his stomach, he wondered if that was how Charles felt when he arrived on the island. There was a mixed feeling of dread and excitement as the plane docked. He grabbed his bag and made his way towards the exit. He walked down the ramp towards the front of the airport. He made his way to a cab that was parked at the curb.

"Hey, I need to find a hotel that is close to the resort, can you help me out?" Jacob asked.

"Absolutely, I know just the place and it's quite secluded." The driver was a young woman, she had an american accent and had dark brown hair. He couldn't see much else of her because of the darkness from the night.

"Thank you miss. I appreciate your help." Said Jacob as he began texting Chuck that he had landed and looking for a place to stay that was close to the resort.

"Happy to help. There is a small cabin near the east side of the resort, the owner is a friend of mine so I can get ya a great deal. You can stay there tonight and tomorrow we can get a rental agreement set up." She said with a very cheerful tone.

"Wow, thank you so much. It must be my lucky day, maybe I can repay your kindness with a drink or dinner while here?" Jacob said in a playful tone.

"Well, there is some good stuff at the cabin, maybe a nightcap for the evening and then we can talk about dinner." She glimpsed back at him and smiled.

With that simple look, Jacob was sure he knew this woman. There was something in her eyes that he couldn't place but was very familiar.

"So, where are you from, if you don't mind me asking? I noticed that you sound American." Jacob tried his best not to sound suspicious of her. While he was asking her that, he began texting Chuck. "If something were to happen to me before we get a chance to meet up, I need you to know a few things. Charles had a son with a woman named Carolyn after he returned from the island. His name was Charles, after his father and Patrick was his middle name. I think somewhere you are a distant relative of theirs." He hit send when the woman replied.

"I used to live stateside a long time ago, why do you ask? The cabin is just up ahead a bit. There is the resort." Her tone had gone from cheerful to a bit more serious.

“Something about you seems familiar, you remind me of someone I used to know.” Jacob replied back to her and continued texting Chuck. “I want you to know that, in my eyes, I see you as I saw Charles. You are family to me and I want nothing more than to see you safe and happy. This thing with Cassandra may not be as easy and clear as we think it is, I believe there is more to this story than we both know.”

“I hope it's someone good and not anyone who may have caused you pain.” She said ominously. The woman was beginning to think that Jacob may just have her confused with someone else, she thought it may be time to have some fun with him.

“Thats an interesting choice of words. It appears that you might just recognize me as well.” Jacob had a terrible feeling in the pit of his stomach as she pulled up to the cabin.

“Well, here we are handsome, this is the cabin my friend rents out to tourists visiting her island as she likes to call it.” She laughed.

"It's a nice looking place, kind of dark, doesn't seem too inviting with all the lights off." Jacob was very leary about getting out of the cab.

"If it'll help, I will go turn on the lights." She got out of the cab and walked to the front door of the house. She went in and turned on the inside lights and the porch light. She stepped out of the doorway and into the light.

Jacob saw that he was mistaken about the woman, he did not know her but something about her was familiar. He sent a quick text to Chuck, "I may have been overreacting about my current situation but nevertheless, what I sent was the truth. Whatever happens during this undertaking we must proceed with caution. I will see you tomorrow night Chuck. Stay safe my friend." He got out of the cab and began walking towards the cabin.

"Is this a little more welcoming for you, sweetness? Now how about that night cap? Come on in and follow me." She said as she turned around and led Jacob to the kitchen.

"A night cap sounds great and maybe we can talk about that dinner." Jacob said as he set his bag down on the kitchen table and smiled at her.

She poured them a drink and handed Jacob his glass. They clinked them together and swallowed the booze down in a gulp. She stepped towards Jacob and kissed him on the lips.

He stepped forward to return the favor and her phone pinged.

“Whoa there cowboy, hold your horses.” She checked her phone and looked up at him. “Sorry, maybe another time, duty calls. Got bills to pay and customers to drive.” She kissed him on the cheek, winked and headed out the door.

Jacob smiled and locked the door behind her. He grabbed his phone, clicked on Chuck's name then the green dial button. He walked over to his bag but stopped when he heard something move in the house. He turned around with claws and teeth extended, fully ready to defend himself from the intruder. He dropped his phone when he saw his intruder, he was frozen in disbelief.

“Hello Jacob!” a familiar woman's voice was the only thing he heard before the intruder pounced on him like a deranged animal. He never had a chance to defend himself. The intruder ripped at his throat spraying blood all over the dining room table and floor. Jacob gasped and choked on his own blood and the intruder drank and drank. Once the intruder stopped, she knelt over him and placed both hands on either side of his head. She leaned down and whispered, "Vengeance is mine." With all her might she pulled on Jacobs head, he tried to scream but no sound came out. She pulled once more, as ligaments tore and his spine snapped, she tore his head off of his body. She held Jacob's severed head over herself and feasted on the dripping blood. She threw the head towards the couch leaving his bloody ravaged corpse in the middle of the room.

"Hello. Jacob, are you there? Are you ok? Please answer me. JACOB!!!" The sound of Chuck yelling for his friend echoed in the house.

The intruder picked up the phone and crushed it in her hand.

Chuck was frantically trying to call Jacob back but each time he tried the line went straight to voicemail. He had tried several times but still got only voicemail. He looked at Christy, who was watching him, in absolute horror as he dropped to his knee.

"No. No. No. This can't be happening, not like this and not to him again. We need to go, I need to go and find him." Chuck was panic-stricken and only wanted to go and find Jacob.

"No, stop Chuck. If this is what you think it is, then it would be stupid to go out there right now. You don't know how strong she is nor the means to stop her. You would be walking straight to your death and I won't let you do that." She went to him and just held him as he sat there shaking in fear and grief.

"I know this will be difficult but we need to keep it together. Tomorrow we need to act like everything is fine so we don't make the others suspicious." She was watching him as he just quietly sat there, not responding or reacting. "Chuck!" She yelled into his ear.

"Right. I…I got it, I understand. I.. uh.. I am going to shower. We still have dinner plans in a little bit. I will get ready." Chuck said in a low monotone voice. He grabbed a change of clothes from his suitcase and headed to the bathroom. He turned on the hot water and as the steam filled the bathroom, tears streamed down his face. He stood there in the shower with the hot water pouring over him, washing the fallen tears away.

Christy had no idea who this Jacob was to Chuck but by the reaction he had, clearly he meant a lot to him. She was at a loss for words and was unsure what to do next. She sat on the edge of the bed and could hear him crying in the shower. She turned the tv on so the others wouldn't be able to hear him. She got up, got undressed and headed to the shower to join him.

Chuck had no idea that Christy was in the bathroom, it wasn't until he felt her arm wrapping around did he realize she was there. She pulled him closer, pressing her warm naked body against his. She could feel his pain, his agony and she just held him tighter. He turned around and placed his head next to hers. She was only a few inches shorter than him so they were almost cheek to cheek. They both formed their heads and kissed each other. He ran his hands down the center of her back, stopping mid way to pull her closer to him. Their bodies glided off of each other from all the water pouring down their bodies. Before they could go any further there was a pounding on the bathroom door.

They were both startled by the loud sudden banging on the door. Chuck stepped out of the shower slowly and cautiously. “Who is it?” He yelled with authority in his voice.

“Calm down Captain love boat. We have to be at the restaurant in a few minutes, so you two need to wrap up whatever is going on in there.” It was Steven reminding them about their dinner reservations.

Chuck looked back at Christy and they both laughed. Chuck handed her a towel and pulled in close for a kiss. “Thank you. You pulled me out of that moment I was having and I truly appreciate you.” He looked at her with a loving glance and hugged her.

She smiled back at him. “You know I'm here for you. No matter what the situation is, I am right here with you.”

“I guess we better get a move on, we have some hungry and impatient people waiting for us.” Chuck laughed as he opened the door to their room exiting the bathroom.

They both got dressed and met the group downstairs. As they walked down the stairs they had snickers and mischievous glances sent their way. Chuck and Christy both exchanged flirtatious smiles and chuckled at their friends.

“OK. Let's go eat.” Chuck announced.

The group made their way downstairs to the resort's restaurant. Chuck knew he had to do everything in his power to keep that gruesome phone call off his mind and make sure everyone enjoys their night.

They started off with some drinks and appetizers. They ordered a plate of bruschetta and gourmet potstickers. They talked, laughed and told embarrassing stories about one another. Once dinner came the chatter subsided for the moment while they ate. Chuck and Steven ordered the filet mignon. Chuck wasn't a fan of the mashed potatoes so he substituted them for rice pilaf. The girls all ordered the grilled chicken breasts with asparagus and the rice pilaf. They ate and one mentioned how good and flavorful the food was. When it came time for dessert the server brought out a tray to choose from. Chuck and Christy chose to share the chocolate mousse cake, Steven had the tiramisu, and Harper and Gloria shared a plate of chocolate covered strawberries. They all ordered another round of drinks and started talking about what their plans were for the morning.

"Honestly, I hope we don't have to get up too early. These drinks are starting to hit me pretty good" Gloria said.

"I was thinking if we got up by nine we could go exploring the island. I looked up this place and saw they have some pretty cool caves and waterfalls." Said Harper.

Steven chimed in. "That actually sounds pretty fun. I'd love a good hike and nature exploration trip."

Chuck knew that he had to find the cave where Charles had taken Cassandra to kill her. If they did that during the day, everyone would be safe. "That sounds good to me." He said as he looked over at Christy.

"Yeah I'm down for that." She was wondering if they were going to find what Chuck was looking for during their exploring. Part of her was hoping they would find something to help them but deep down she also hoped they didn't. The thought of any of them getting hurt worried her more than anything.

Chuck looked over at the waiter and nodded. Then a group of servers came over with a cake and lit candles and began singing happy birthday to Harper and Gloria. The girls looked confused and embarrassed. When the serving staff finished everyone in the restaurant began clapping.

The girls looked at Steven who looked just as confused as them. Then they looked at Chuck who was barely able to contain his laughter.

"I believe there was a bet that was still up in the air for a winner. I think it's safe to say that the title of best prankster remains with the king. Happy Birthday ladies." Chuck said as he was laughing.

Steven and Christy began laughing as well, while Harper and Gloria sat there embarrassed and stuck with a huge slice of cake. They blew out the candles and passed the cake around for all to enjoy. Steven reached over and gave Chuck a fist bump.

"All hail the king." Steven said while laughing and taking a scoop of the cake. "Damn. That's some good cake."

Gloria and Harper, using their hands, made a bowing motion in Chuck's direction.

"Well, played your majesty. I completely forgot about that bet." Gloria said with a little humorous attitude in her voice.

"I was kinda hoping everyone forgot about it. I suck at pranks so I was ok with an even tie." Harper said.

Christy was still giggling from the prank. "When did you have time to tell them to come out and sing happy birthday?"

"I arranged that when I made the reservation. We always did goofy stuff like that when I was a kid. My parents always got me, my sister and sometimes my dad got my mom. The fact that the bet got made was pure coincidence. It's always good to end the night with a good laugh, especially with people you love and care about." Chuck got a little watery eyed because he began to think about Jacob and the messages that he had sent him.

Christy put her hand on his, he smiled and squoze her hand. "We love ya too, you big softy." She tried to make him laugh to get his mind off whatever he was thinking about.

All of a sudden, the restaurant was silenced by the sound of sirens from emergency vehicles that flew past the resort. Chuck's face turned white as a ghost as he spun around in his chair listening to the sounds of the sirens. He knew where they were going and why they were going there. They were headed past the east side of the resort, which is exactly where Jacob said he was going to be staying.

“Well on that note, I think we should call it a night.” Steven said as he saw the expression on his cousin's face.

“Yeah, I… I think that's a good idea. We have to be up somewhat early and we wouldn't wanna miss out on exploring the island tomorrow.” Chuck said with a sound of despair in his voice.

The server brought the check over and Chuck paid it. They all looked at him confused, knowing that the check was going to be high.

“Ummm cuz, we could have split that one. Let me send you some money to your cashapp.” Steven said quickly.

“No, this one is on me. You guys can get the next one, I wanted to do something nice for everyone.” Chuck smiled as he signed the check and put his card away.

“No, seriously let us send you some money Chuck. That's way too much.” Harper said.

“No guys, seriously, I got this one. Don't worry about it.” Chuck said a little more seriously this time.

“Just for the record, you have already done so much for us by booking this trip and the flights. We don't take that lightly, we really appreciate it and we really appreciate you.” Gloria said, smiling at Chuck.

“It's no biggie. I just hope we can do more stuff like this when we get back from vacation. I know this is our last big hoorah before we officially enter the real world with our big jobs and all, it means a lot to me that we are all here and able to do this.” He said wholeheartedly.

They all picked up what was left of their drinks and clinked the glasses to each other before finishing them and leaving the restaurant. They made their way back to the cabin and went to their rooms. Chuck and Christy could hear Steven and Gloria giggling and laughing. Harper even yelled for them to be quiet and go to sleep.

Chuck laid there with his hand behind his head thinking about that phone call he had received before dinner. He thought about the emergency vehicles racing past the resort and wondered what they would find. He knew someone, more than likely Cassandra, had attacked

Jacob and killed him. The gurgling sounds of Jacob choking on his own blood haunted Chuck's mind. He had never heard something so awful and spine tingling in his whole life.

When Christy came to bed, she snuggled up next to Chuck and laid her head on his chest. He wrapped his arm around her and they fell asleep. Maybe it was the alcohol or maybe it was because he was on the island now, but he didn't dream. There was no Cassandra haunting him nor any flashes from the past. Just the cold dark void of emptiness.

When they woke up Chuck felt as if he had barely gotten any rest. Yes, he did sleep, but it wasn't the restful sleep one needs to have the motivation to get out of bed. What got him out of bed was the fact that today was the day he was going to find the cave where Charles failed to end Cassandra. He would find out what he needed to do to finally put an end to this murderous evil creature.

Christy was already up and out of bed. She had gone downstairs and made a trip with the girls to the breakfast buffet the resort offered. She got Chuck a ham and egg omelet, breakfast sausage and a cup of coffee. The girls got themselves some bagels, fruit and coffee. Gloria got Steven a couple of their handmade donuts, she knew he always had sweets for breakfast, and a cup of coffee. The friends ate breakfast quickly and got ready for their day of exploring.

As they were finishing up getting what they were gonna need, Chuck called his new friend Ruben the taxi driver and island expert. “Good morning Ruben. This is Chuck, you gave us a ride from the airport to the resort yesterday. I was wondering if you would be up to driving us around the island today. We were hoping to do some exploring and see some of the island's caves.”

“Ah yes, good morning my friend. I would love to show you all around. Are you looking for anything special? I know the caves and some beautiful waterfalls. Very romantic places.” Ruben responded excitedly.

“Well since you asked, I read the island has an interesting urban legend about vampires, is that true?” Chuck asked.

“Si, si. There is a cave called the tomb where supposedly one was trapped and left to die. I think this was a woman vampira. Would you like to go see this one?” Ruben asked Chuck.

“Yes but I need to ask a favor. Please do not say anything about the vampire part to my friends, they think I'm loco because I like vampire stories.” Chuck laughed trying to play off the fact that this was only a small portion of the truth.

Ruben laughed as well. “Ok, my friend. I no tell them anything about la vampira. It will be secret between you and me. I will leave my home now and see you all soon. Thank you for calling amigo.” Ruban hung up the phone.

Chuck went over to the group, “Ok our very own island expert is on his way to take us to some cool caves and some beautiful romantic waterfalls. His words not mine.”

They all snickered and grabbed their bookbags. They headed downstairs to wait for Ruben to pick them up. Chuck went over to the concierge desk. “Good morning. I was wondering if you knew why all those emergency vehicles were speeding past the resort last night.”

“Good morning. I hope the cabin is working to your liking and dinner was enjoyable. The emergency vehicles from last night were going to the scene of a horrific tragedy. A young man was found murdered last night. When the owner of the home had returned from work, she found the man." The concierge manager leaned forward towards Chuck to whisper. "The young man was decapitated. It was a grisly scene, nothing like this has ever happened before. It has some of the residents concerned that a tourist was responsible. Please try to keep this to yourself, I do not want to create a panic for the guests of the resort."

Chuck stammered. "Right. Absolutely. I will keep that to myself and I hope they catch whoever is responsible for hurting that poor young man. Thank you for the update."

Ruben had pulled up to the resort and he hurried over to let them know he had arrived. "Hello my friends. Who is ready for some exploring? I take you to all the best places I know about."

The group cheered and eagerly climbed into Rubens minivan. He began to drive east of the resort. Chuck looked out the window as they drove by a house with several police cars parked in the driveway. There was a woman crying while sitting on the front steps of the house.

"Hey Ruben, do you know what happened at that house last night? We heard a bunch of sirens and vehicles flying past the resort last night?" Steven asked.

"I hear that a man was badly injured but nothing else. I have a friend who works for the policia, so soon I'm sure she will tell me what happened." Ruben replied.

"If we are still here when you find out can you let us know? I am curious what the commotion was all about." Steven said.

"Yes, when she tells me I call and let you know. Do you want to see waterfalls first or caves.?" Ruben quickly changed the subject to something more exciting and not so depressing.

"Let's go see the waterfalls before it gets too hot out, it'll be cooler in the caves so it makes sense to see those when it's hotter." Harper said.

The group agreed, but Chuck remained silent. He was thinking about the terrible way that Jacob died. He now knew that the gurgling sound was Jacob choking on his own blood as he was being brutally attacked and decapitated. Shivers ran down his back and he felt nauseous for a moment. He saw Christy looking over at him and he smiled at her. He knew that sooner or later he would have to tell her who Jacob was, but right now he needed to focus on what was going on in the moment.

Ruben had slowed down the van. "Down this path is a beautiful waterfall, locals call it the lover's getaway. We get out and I take you to go see it."

They all piled out of the van and began following Ruben down a well laid path. It was about a mile away from the main road. When they reached the waterfall, everyone gazed in amazement and cheered together.

"Are we allowed to get in the water?" Gloria asked Ruben.

"Yes, of course. Go and have fun." Ruben said laughing.

They all ran towards that waterfall. The girls stripped down to their swimsuits and jumped in. Chuck and Steven wanted to go and climb the rock along the waterfall. Christy yelled for them to be careful.

As they approached the rocky wall of the waterfall, Chuck thought he saw something moving behind the wall of water. He walked along the edge of the rocks until he got directly behind the waterfall. He looked around but didn't see anything initially, then he heard a rustling noise further back in the small cave. He took a few steps towards the noise but let out a short yelp as a small group of bats flew over his head and out of the cave. He began laughing and made his way back to the group. Steven had already climbed to the top of the waterfall, he was peeking down over the ledge. Then he jumped.

Steven let out a loud, “woooooo” as he jumped and he made a big splash as he hit the water. Gloria yelled at him for jumping as she swam over to him. He popped out of the water laughing and grabbed Gloria and pulled her under the water. They both came up laughing and kissed. Chuck walked over towards Christy and sat next to her at the edge of the water.

“So, I owe you an explanation about that call I got last night. It was a friend of mine and Charles’s from when Charles was alive. He was turned into a vampire by Cassandra when she tried to kill him. He had survived throughout the years but because of me and these damn nightmares, he is now dead. The concierge said that a young man was murdered and decapitated last night. That was Jacob, Cassandra got to him and killed him before he could help us." Chuck told her more of Jacob's past with Charles and how Charles kept him from going with him to the island in order to keep him safe.

Christy, now fully aware of what Chuck was feeling last night, looked down as a few tears rolled down her face for his friend. Chuck did for her what she did for him, he grabbed her and hugged her tight.

"We can't mourn for Jacob just yet, if the others see either of us crying they will get suspicious and start asking questions. When we finish this, we will mourn for him and for everyone who has fallen prey to this murderous bitch." Chuck said with a strong sense of determination.

"Ok, you're right. Maybe we should head to the next waterfall. Get this show movin." Christy said as she splashed some water on her face to wash away the tears and refresh herself.

Over the next few hours Ruben took them to a few more waterfalls. The group had so much fun and took so many pictures. Steven made a point of climbing each waterfall and jumping off the ledge, he even got Chuck to jump off a couple of them. The girls were happy just to be splashing around and working on their tans. After the last waterfall, they stopped for lunch and as a thank you to Ruben they bought him lunch.

“Are you ready to go cave exploring now?” Ruben asked them as they finished their lunches.

“Definitely. Right, guys?” Chuck asked excitedly.

The group all yelled yeah in unison.

“Ok. There are three really cool caves that are easy to get to, some of the other ones require professionals because you have to go underwater to get to them. I am expert of the island but not swimming, those are too dangerous for me.” Ruben said as they all walked back to his van.

“The three you know about will be good, we aren’t prepared for underwater caves. Though, that does sound fun, but maybe for another day.” Chuck said, trying not to sound too eager to get going.

“OK, let's go.” Ruben said as he started the van.

The first two caves were amazing with bats hanging high above them, cave crickets that looked like giant spiders and amazing structures in each. By the time they got to the last cave, which was the one Chuck had been waiting for, it was going on four o'clock. The day had started cooling off and the shaded areas were slowly spreading.

This cave is at the end of the beach, Ruben said as they walk along an all too familiar shoreline. Chuck began to get anxious because he had been on this beach several times in his dreams and each time he was there so was Cassandra. As they approached the cave there was a sinister feeling in the air, Chuck noticed it first and then Ruben did. He looked at Chuck, as if to tell him this was the cave he was asking about. Chuck nodded to him as they approached the entrance.

"I wait here for you, my leg is giving me pain. I wait at the logs by where they light fires at night. You go in, explore and have fun." Ruben slowly walked back to the logs where Chuck had spoken to Cassandra a few times.

"What? You don't want to come in with us?" Christy asked Ruben nervously.

"No thank you. I need to rest my legs. Go, I will be waiting here for you." He said smiling at her trying to ease her nerves.

Chuck went in first, with a flash of a small memory, he walked straight towards a smaller cavern within the cave. Christy stayed close to him while the others went further into the cave to look around.

Chuck stopped at the entrance of the small cavern, took out his phone and turned on the light. He didn't want to take any chances and miss something that could be important. Christy moved closer to him, holding his arm tight. She whispered "be careful."

He looked at her and nodded. They stepped into the cavern and began looking around.

Steven and the girls went their own way, and further towards the back of the main cave. As they moved slowly, Harper saw something laying on the floor. She stepped away from Steven and Gloria as they continued further into the cave. She bent down to pick up the object and inspected it. It was a necklace but it looked new, it was made out of gold. It was a gold chain and had a rose pendant. The pendant looked as if it was made out of some type of gemstone.

"Oh, you found my necklace." Said a young woman who had stepped out of the shadows.

Harper was startled by the woman, she had jumped and dropped the necklace. “Holy crap, you scared me!” Harper said.

“I am so sorry, I didn't mean to. I was exploring earlier with my friends and I fell. When I got up I noticed my necklace had come off. I've been meaning to get that clasp fixed but keep forgetting, it was a gift and I was so scared that I wouldn't find it. You are my hero.” The woman spoke with a soft, kind tone.

Harper looked at the necklace and saw the clasp was stuck open. She handed it to the woman and smiled. “I’m glad I was able to find it for you, I know I would be upset too if I lost something that pretty.”

“I am so grateful, here let me give you some money for finding it for me.” The woman said.

“Please, no, keep your money. I am just happy I could do something nice for someone, even if it was an accidental find.” Harper said, smiling at the woman.

“Can I at least give you a hug? You have no idea how much this necklace means to me.” The woman said with a sound of sadness in her voice.

“OK. I can take a hug.” Harper said sweetly.

As Harper stepped closer to the woman, there was an odd gleam in her eyes. Kind of like the reflection you see when an animal is staring at you in the night. Before Harper could step back the woman threw her arms around her and gave her a big squeeze. Harper tried to let go but the woman pulled her closer and held on tighter.

The woman whispered in Harper's ear. “This isn’t your fault but you will suffer because of him.” Then the woman pulled Harper further into the dark as she covered Harper's mouth to keep her from yelling for help.

Before Harper could do anything she felt a tinge of pain on her shoulder, she began to fall to the ground and then everything went dark. The woman had sunk her sharp pointed teeth into Harper's shoulder, then she bit her own wrist and dripped blood into Harper's mouth. As Harper gasped in pain, she began drinking down something warm, she did not know she was swallowing the woman's blood. The woman wiped Harper's face clean and watched as the bite marks slowly faded into scars. Then she disappeared into the darkness of the cave.

While all this was going on, Chuck and Christy had made their own shocking discovery. As they searched the cavern, Chuck stumbled over something small and round on the floor of the cave. Chuck shined his light on the object and saw it was a decayed piece of wood. As he looked closer he noticed the piece of wood came to a point, it was a wooden stake. They looked around where they were standing and there were several more stakes scattered on the floor. One of the stakes was standing erect as if it was stuck in something. Chuck moved closer to where the stake was standing and was shocked to see it sticking out of a skeleton.

He looked at Christy in disbelief and horror. Christy walked over to where Chuck was kneeling and looked at the skeleton. It laid there, fully decomposed so that the bones were the only thing that remained. As Chuck ran his light up the bones, he stopped at the sternum where a stake had clearly pierced the heart of its victim. The stake went all the way down to the ground. The light was steadily shaking as he moved it further up the skeleton to the skull, revealing a blood curdling reality, this was Cassandra's skeleton. He could tell it was her by the two fangs that were on the top row of teeth of the decayed skeleton. Charles didn’t fail in his quest to end her horrifying reign of terror.

Chuck looked at Christy once more, struggling to get the words out, he finally spoke. "These are Cassandra's bones. If this is Cassandra, who has been tormenting me and haunting me. What is going on?"

Chapter Ten

Chuck was in utter dismay as he realized that he and Christy were looking at the bones of the woman that had been haunting and tormenting him since they started this nightmare vacation. This meant that Charles did not fail in ending Cassandra's evil reign of terror but someone had picked up where she left off. Someone knew that he and Charles shared a connection and they intended on exploiting that connection but for what purpose.

Chuck's thoughts and confusion were interrupted by a piercing shriek that echoed off the walls of the cave shattering the silence. Both he and Christy ran out of the cave to see what was going on. It was Harper, she was moving erratically, clutching her shoulder and crying. Gloria ran towards her but was met with an unearthly strong shove from her sister. She, like Charles had done, flew into the wall of the cave. Harper, realizing what she had done, ran to her sister. Steven ran over as well, put his hand on Harper's shoulder and asked if she was ok.

Harper screamed and swung her hand back, her hand which now had claws in place of finger nails. Those claws tore through Stevens chest and right arms like a hot knife through butter. Steven fell to the ground, bleeding from the wounds that Harper had made. Harper cried even harder, unable to control herself or her monstrous abilities.

Steven cried out in pain. "Harper, what the fuck is wrong with you? Get away from Gloria!" He demanded of her.

Gloria moaned on the ground as she was slowly regaining consciousness. "Wha…what happened? Harper, what happened?" She tried to roll towards her sister but Harper jumped back and landed with her feet on the wall of the cave.

Harper was bewildered at the fact that she was quite literally sitting on the wall of the cave. She slowly put her feet on the ground and lowered herself into a crouching position. She sobbed uncontrollably and stared directly at Chuck. She stood up slowly, took a step towards him and pointed at him.

"You. This, all of this, is your fault. She said so. She said this was because of you. You knew all along didn't you? You and Christy, you both knew all of it was real. Your psychotic sounding dreams, they weren't dreams at all. She was setting the traps and you fell for all of them." Harper was beginning to see flashes of the woman's plan, it was in her blood and now it was in Harpers. "You and your idiotic obsession with vampires. If you had only known it was because of Charles and Cassandra." Her voice began to get deeper, turning into a raspy and angry growl.

Chuck stepped directly in front of Christy. "Harper, you're right. It is all my fault. I've always had this dumb obsession with vampires and didn't know why until we left for this vacation. I didn't want to say anything because deep down I was hoping I was just crazy. I never wanted anyone to get hurt, I am so sorry. But I have to ask you, Harper, do you know who bit you?" He hated having to ask her but he had to know.

"That's all you care about, isn't it? Getting your revenge? You really are just like him." Harper began creeping towards Chuck, she had a snarl on her face and her clawed hands at her side.

"Yes, I am like him because I will do whatever I need to do to protect the people I love. He died knowing that his life meant very little in comparison to those he loved and lost because of her." Chuck started moving himself and Christy towards the cave's entrance, he could see that Ruben was still out there and trying to see what was going on from a distance.

"Harper, please don't hurt anyone else. We love you so much, please stop this." Christy called out to her friend.

"You're just as guilty as he is. You hid the fact that you knew he was telling the truth this whole time. I bet you even knew about his secret helper, didn't you?" Harper asked as she got closer and closer to them.

"No, I didn't know about him til this morning when Chuck found out he was murdered." Christy said while Chuck continued to move them closer to the entrance.

"Help us Harper. Help me stop whoever is doing this. You have the choice on what kind of person you want to become. You don't have to be like the one who bit you or like Cassandra." Chuck pleaded with her as he and Christy stopped at the mouth of the cave.

"I'm nothing like any of you." Harper screamed. In her head she heard the voice of the woman who bit her speak to her. "KILL HIM!!!" The voice screamed and Harper charged directly at Chuck.

She hit him so hard that they both flew out of the cave. Chuck was able to get his feet up between himself and Harper. The moment they hit the sand they rolled back just enough for him to kick her off of him. With the momentum from the land and him kicking up with all his might, she flew back a few feet. She began screaming out in agony because the sun was still up. She rolled and kicked in the sand but it was no use, the sun poured over her like napalm covering the ground.

Christy ran out of the cave and was headed straight towards her burning friend. "Harper!!! No, someone help!!!"

Chuck grabbed her, pulling her to the ground. "Christy, stop. There isn't anything you can do to help her. That fire can't be extinguished." He said with tears rolling down his face.

Gloria was the next one to run towards Harper. Chuck and Christy couldn't grab her in time and Steven was too far behind her to catch her. She reached down for her sister, hoping to roll her body in the sand, and scream out in pain. She fell to the floor crying her sister's name. Her left forearm and hand were covered in burns. The fire was so hot that parts of her skin blistered instantly and some areas of the skin turned completely white. Steven picked her up and carried her to the water.

Ruben stood there frozen with fear. He looked at the four remaining friends and then he looked at the sun. It was barely peaking over the ocean when he looked at Chuck in terror. As he looked at the entrance of the cave, he started walking backwards and praying loudly. All of a sudden something flew out of the cave and right at him. Ruben fell to the ground, blood pouring out of his neck and pooling in the sand.

"Who was that Chuck?" Christy asked him.

"I don't know. I wish I did but I honestly have no idea who we are dealing with." He said with fear in his voice.

Steven's shirt was covered in his blood, using the only free hand he had he helped Gloria up and then tried putting pressure on his own wounds. Gloria glared at Chuck and Christy as she walked towards them. Steven spoke first. "We need to get to a hospital, like now."

"Is it true? What Harper had said, that you both knew that this vampire shit was real and not just something from Chuck's warped little mind." Gloria was furious and still had tears streaming down her face. As she looked down, all that was left of what was once her sister was a pile of smoldering ashes.

"We had no way of knowing that what was happening was real. I'm sorry to say this but part of me was hoping that maybe Chuck was having a psychotic break." She looked at Chuck with sadness in her eyes. "I'm sorry. I don't know what else to say except I'm sorry."

"I believed it was true." Chuck said. "The nightmares, the visions of a past life and the vampires. I believed all of it and part of me wanted it all to be a lie. How could something so far-fetched and supernatural be real? It was only real in the movies or on TV. But from what I've seen, the movies and TV had some of it right. I know how to beat her and end her for good. I am truly sorry I brought you all into this. I wouldn't blame any of you if you left me to deal with this alone. I deserve that." He spoke with heart break and remorse.

Christy grabbed his hand and squoze it tight. "I said I was with you til the end, whether it was real or not, I still am right here. Let's get them to a hospital, after that we find this evil bitch and end her."

"OK. I will get the keys from Ruben." Chuck walked over to where Ruben was laying in a pool of his own blood. He stood there looking at the poor man who only wanted to drive them around and help him out. He knew it was his fault, he asked Ruben about that damn cursed cave and asked him to take them to it. "I am so sorry, Ruben." He whispered as he grabbed the keys out of his pants pocket.

Chuck turned away from Rubens corpse and ran over to the others. They were already walking to the van, Chuck hit the unlock button on the remote and they all climbed in. He drove in the direction of the resort and was pressing hard on the gas pedal. They got back to the resort and Chuck ran inside to get directions to the nearest hospital. He got back into the van and hit the gas so hard that the tires spun and screeched as they took off.

They arrived at the hospital, Steven and Gloria got out and went straight inside the emergency room. Chuck and Christy left the moment that the doors closed behind them. "They will be safe there." Chuck said as he drove back to the resort.

“We need to figure out where she could be hiding and we need weapons. There was a wooden stake in the cave in Cassandra's skeleton, so we know that those work. Sunlight is a definite way to stop her but we have a long time til sunrise. The only other things that I can think of are Holy water and silver.” Chuck said as he pulled up to the resort.

Christy sat there looking at him, wondering how he was being so calm in this nightmare of a situation. “The gift shop.” She blurted out. “I bet they have silver. They sell jewelry and I am willing to bet some of it is made from silver. As far as finding holy water, maybe the resort has a church in it or nearby.”

They both got out of the van and made their way to the gift shop. They began looking at the jewelry and found only a few things made from silver. “Excuse me ma’am, do you have anything else that is made with silver?” Christy asked the gift shop clerk.

“We have some silver souvenir spoons and the rings that you are looking at, that's about it. Would you like to see any of the rings?” The clerk asked.

“We’ll take them all and the spoons.” Chuck said quickly.

“What? All of them? Are you sure?” The clerk stumbled over his own words.

“You heard the man. Bag them up. Here’s a credit card to charge it to.” Christy had handed the man the first card she could find in her purse, sadly it was Harpers.

The clerk rang up the items and bagged them up. He handed Christy the bag and credit card, “Have a good day and thank you for your business.”

They hurried off to their cabin to make some kind of weapon out of the stuff they just bought. Outside of the cabin was a pile of logs for the fire pit, Chuck grabbed a few of those and brought them inside. They sat down for a moment and took a breath. Chuck brought them a glass of water each and they got to work,

Chuck grabbed a knife and began carving the logs. He put the knife down in frustration and walked out to the wood pile. He came back in with the axe that was sitting next to the pile of logs and used it to chip away at the logs. He went through four logs and made oddly shaped stakes. He looked at the stakes and then looked at the axe. “I think

I'll keep the axe handy with these ridiculous looking stakes." He said out loud.

Christy took the silver spoons and started pounding on them with a hammer she found in the closet. She was able to flatten the spoons and then she started scratching them on a rock she had brought in. She hit her finger on the rock and threw the spoon on the floor. "This is stupid, I can't do anything with these damn spoons. The most I can do is maybe make it so they can fit around a could of fingers like some goofy brass knuckles. It is stupid." She was feeling defeated and tired.

"Hey, we will have to take what we can get. If that is all we can make with those then so be it. We will make it work, we have to make it work. For Harper, Steven, Gloria and Ruben. We need to make it work." He said with tears in his eyes.

Christy walked over to him and hugged him. She just held him quietly and kissed him on the forehead. "We will make this work Chuck and we will do this together. We need to sleep too. We can not keep at this and continue while running on fumes."

"You're right. We should take shifts, I will keep watch first. You can go lay down. I will keep working on these stakes and try to find out where she could be hiding." Chuck said to Christy as he walked her over to the couch.

"OK but don't let me be the only one who gets sleep. You need to sleep as well. Plus, your dreams seem to be linked to whoever this is, whether it's Cassandra or not." Christy said to a tired Chuck.

Chuck knew that she was making a very good point. Whoever was behind his nightmares, both asleep and awake, they knew him very well. Chuck needed to prepare himself for a possible confrontation in his dreams. One thing that puzzled him, as he watched over Christy, whoever was behind this madness offered him the chance at immortality. The same offer that Cassandra made Charles. So, either those weren't Cassandra's bones and she somehow survived Charles's attack or someone is in some way impersonating Cassandra and playing out her life.

Chuck walked around the cabin, checking all the rooms and making sure all the doors and windows were locked. He made some coffee and poured himself a cup. He sat in one of the chairs at the table and sipped on his coffee.

He was startled when someone knocked on the door. He picked up the axe and walked over to the door.

"Who is it?" He called out as he moved closer to the door.

"Room service sir. The manager sent over a bottle of champagne as a thank you for your large purchase in the gift shop." The voice belonged to a woman and that made Chuck nervous.

"Thank you. That's very kind but could you please leave it at the door? I am not currently dressed." He said and peeked out of the peep hole on the door. He could barely make out the woman standing there. It was as if the shadows moved for her to keep her identity a secret from the light.

"Are you certain that you want me to leave the bottle on the ground? Someone may steal it, I would hate for that to happen." The woman questioned his decision.

"I'm quite certain miss. It won't be out there for long, I just need to put some clothes on and I will bring it in." He said a bit more sternly.

The woman laughed. “No need to get aggressive my dear. I was simply trying to be helpful. It's not like I was asking you to invite me in or anything. Sweet dreams Chuck.”

He instantly recognized the voice, it was Cassandra’s voice. He ran over to Christy and woke her up. “It’s Cassandra, she was just outside of the front door.”

Christy sprang up from the couch that she was fast asleep on. “What? Are you sure it was her?” She asked sleepily as she made her way to the front door.

He handed her one of the stakes and he grabbed the axe. “Stay behind me.” He whispered to her.

He slowly opened the door and peaked out into the night. He couldn’t see anything except for the bottle of Champagne. He picked it up, brought it inside and quickly locked the door behind him. He walked over and set the bottle down on the table. “She left that outside our door. She pretended to be a worker and tried to get me to open the door.” He sounded frantic while he explained what had happened.

“But why would she pose as an employee just to get you to open the door. Couldn’t she have just barged her way in here without even breaking a sweat?" Christy asked, confused by what he had just explained to her.

"I guess not, in some of the vampire stuff I've seen they need to be invited in. They just can't come barging in, I don't know why but that's what I've seen and read." Chuck stated with some certainty.

"Babe, you need some sleep." Christy said as she led him to the couch where she had been sleeping.

"Yes I do, I do need some sleep." He said as he laid on the couch.

Christy pulled the blanket up and over his shoulders. She sat at the table and made herself a cup of coffee from the pot that he had made. She sat there sipping the coffee and looking at the bottle of champagne that was left on their doorstep.

Chuck had drifted off to sleep quickly. He was exhausted from the craziness of the day and he was emotionally drained. He heard the knocking at the door again and he got up to answer it. He saw Christy was still sitting at the table but she had fallen asleep. Her head rested gently on her arms and he could hear her soft snoring. He continued to the door and opened it. Before he could stop himself he stepped out of the doorway and fell.

He was surprised to see that he landed on sand. He pushed himself up and saw lots of sand. He looked around and he was on that damn beach again. He rushed to his feet and started looking around. Ruben's body was gone and so was Harper's burnt remains. Chuck started walking over to the cave, cautiously looking around and waiting for her to make her presence known.

He had just reached the entrance of the cave and he heard her voice.

"Hello Chuck." Cassandra said with some humor in her voice. "Did you not like the bottle of champagne I left for you?"

"You're not Cassandra. I don't know who you are but I saw her bones in that cave and there was a stake sticking out of where the heart would have been." Chuck said as he was pointing to the entrance of the cave.

She laughed at him. "How can you tell me who I am and who I am not? I have lived for hundreds of years, I think I know who I am. Perhaps you're the one forgetting who you are. Are you a man who lived in the 1800s or are you living in the 2000s? Are you really hunting a vampire or have you finally lost your mind and are hallucinating this whole thing? Maybe you are actually locked in a psychiatric hospital and none of this is real? How can you tell?" She stared into his eyes, making him question his reality and her existence.

Chuck stood there quietly. He looked at the sand beneath his feet, he felt the breeze and the mist of the ocean on his face. Her words echoed in his head as he remained there in silence. He looked up at her as she stood there smiling, then he smiled. "You're right. How do I know that I am not just having a mental breakdown? Maybe after all the years and stresses of school and life, I've finally snapped. But if that's the case then you must not be real and if you're not real then there is nothing to be afraid of. You could just be a figment of my imagination, something I created to talk to. If that's the case then you have no true power and you're not some big scary monster. You are just a ghost, a mirage and you're nothing." He smirked, turned his back to her and started walking into the cave. If she was "real" then he knew what he just did would make her angry and when you're angry you make mistakes.

She watched him walk into the cave and her blood began to boil. “Don’t turn you back on me, you pathetic piece of meat.” She screamed at him as he walked away from her. She charged at him and pushed him further into the cave. “You think you’re so smart but you have no idea who you are messing with.” She kicked him in the gut, sending him rolling into the cavern where he had found Cassandra's bones.

He laid there laughing in pain. “Sure, I do, you’re probably something I created to rub one out to. I mean look at you.” He coughed as he crawled his way over to the bones. “You have a great body, nice rack and I do have a strange obsession with vampires. So, yeah, you are probably something my mind made up to keep my obsession satisfied. After all, there are no such things as vampires or monsters.” He reached for one of the bones to use as a weapon against her but another well placed kick sent him into the wall and he crashed down on top of the bones.

“You disgusting, filthy piece of garbage. Why anyone would waste time and effort on you is a miracle. You don’t deserve to live, let alone be given the opportunity of immortality. These bones have more meaning than you." She growled at him as she circled him while he laid in the pile of crushed bones.

"Actually, I've been meaning to ask you about that." He coughed again, he was able to make it up to his knees and he looked at her. "Why did you offer to turn me? I mean Charles had the sense to refuse you countless times, what made you think I would do anything different?" He reached down to the ground to push himself on to his feet, he felt something under his hand and slid it into his pocket as he stood up.

"Foolish sentiment on my part. To think, at one point in time you were deserving of such a gift. I don't know why she would have offered it to you, you should have been a meal after..." She stopped and looked at him, realizing she had said too much and she screamed at him.

Chuck caught that slip she had just made and he smiled. "She? So, I was right, you're not her. You're not Cassandra and this pile of dust is what remains of her." He looked down and kicked the bones that remained at his feet. "What were you gonna say? I should have been a meal after what?"

“After she killed Jacob, she should have killed you. She should never have wasted her time trying to convince him to spend eternity with her. If you, he, truly loved her there should never have been a hesitation. It was selfishness on his part. He was a coward.” The woman yelled in Chuck's face.

Chuck could feel his own anger building up inside of him, he took a breath and tried to keep it at bay. “Charles was many things but he was not a coward. He sacrificed himself for the sake of countless others, people like Jacob, innocent people that were on the wrong side of a monstrous woman.” He said to the woman.

“Oh yes, he was so noble. He protected so many people, except for the ones he was supposed to protect. He even had the nerve to replace her after he murdered her on this godforsaken island.” She was tired of talking, she lunged at Chuck and grabbed him by the throat pinning him against the cave wall. “Enough of this, let's see if when you die here, will you die out there.”

She growled at him and tightened the grip she had around his neck. She started lifting him up off the ground with one hand. He reached up to grab her arm and she pinned it to the wall. Doing that caused her to move her entire body closer to his. He gasped for air and tried to say something to her. She leaned in closer to try and make out what he was saying. Chuck reached into his pocket and pulled out what he had felt under his hand after she kicked him, the wooden stake. He plunged it into her side, pushing it in as far as he could make it go.

The woman screamed in pain and let go of Chuck's throat. She tried to reach for the stake to pull it out of her side but she couldn't reach it. Chuck, who was gasping for air on the ground, crawled over to the woman. Her screams and wails echoed off the walls of the cave reaching to the darkest parts. A horde of bats came flying out of a hole in the wall and Chuck rolled away from them. They chased him out of the cave and as he jumped though the opening, he shot up from the couch that he had fallen asleep on.

He sat up gasping for air and clutching his side where he had been kicked in the dream. Christy, who had fallen asleep at the end of the couch next to him, was startled awake but his gasps. Chuck fell on the floor coughing as Christy rushed to his side. She helped him up to his feet and over to the table. She hurried over to the fridge and grabbed him a cold water bottle. She opened it, handed it to him and he quickly chugged it down.

“What the hell just happened Chuck?” Christy asked him. She had a look of fear, confusion and concern on her face.

“I…I think I know where she is.” He stuttered. He sat there for a moment quietly going over what had just happened in his head.

“Chuck!!!” Christy shouted. She watched him jump and he looked at her. “What happened?”

“Sorry. It's not her, it’s not Cassandra. Whoever she is, she let it slip that she wasn’t Cassandra but she knows all about her and Charles.” Chuck got quiet again but not for long. “There is a hole in the wall in the cave, I think that is where she’s hiding during the day. I hurt her in my dream but I’m not sure if it did anything to her out here.”

Christy looked over at the window and could see that the sun was already starting to rise. “Well, at least we have the sun on our side. We should get moving while it's early, use as much of this daylight to our advantage.” Christy was much more comfortable searching for this woman during the day.

“OK. I wanna change my clothes really quick. I promise I won’t take long.” Chuck said as he made his way upstairs to their room. He grabbed his suitcase and threw it on the bed. He put on a clean shirt and a pair of jeans. As he was rummaging around his bag looking for socks something fell out and hit the floor. He quickly grabbed it, put it in his back pocket and put his socks and shoes on.

Christy was impatiently waiting for him by the door. “Are you ready?” She said exhaustedly.

“Yep lets get moving.” Chuck said as he grabbed the keys to Ruben’s van and headed out the door.

“Should we stop at the ER to check on Steven and Gloria?” She asked as she buckled her seat belt.

“No, not yet. They’re probably still pissed off at us. If we come back after we've finished this, they might be a bit more forgiving.” He started the van and drove to the cave.

“Ok, that's a good idea.” Christy watched out the window as they sped past the house where Jacob was killed.

As they approached the beach, they expected cops or tons of people crowded around Ruben's body or Harper's ashes. There was no one in sight, no bloody corpse and no pile of ashes. Chuck parked the van up the street from the beach and put the keys in the glove box. Christy looked at him confused.

"I don't wanna lose them in a dark cave." He said and laughed.

Christy smirked and rolled her eyes. "Let's check the back for flashlights or something to give us some light so we're not completely blind in there."

Chuck popped the back hatch door open and was surprised to find a box of glowsticks and a flashlight. "Hey check this out." He called Christy over to show her his find. "Ruben must have been a better cave explorer than he let on."

Christy started filling her pockets with the glow sticks and Chuck did the same. He handed her the flashlight, he picked up the stakes and the axe. She closed the hatch and they began walking to the beach. As they briskly made their way down the street, they left behind everything they once knew. People they knew and loved had either been torn from them, turned on them or stolen from their lives. They knew that if they survived nothing would ever be the same. The most unfortunate part of the current situation was that best friends wouldn't have been enough to see them through but they had become more than best friends.

Christy followed Chuck to the small cavern where he picked up the stake that killed Cassandra. He placed it in the pocket opposite of the one he used in the dream. He noticed Christy watching him and he quietly explained what happened in the dream he had at the cabin. She nodded and they pressed on.

Chuck found the hole that the bats had flown out of in his dream. It wasn't big enough for them to crawl through but it meant that there was another way. Christy clicked on the flashlight and saw that the cave wall curved around to a narrow path. Chuck went first, Christy handed him a glowstick she had just cracked. They had to place their backs against the wall and move sideways to get through the passageway. There was a foul odor haunting the air.

They cleared the narrow passage and it let out into a wide open chamber. A few steps in and they saw what was causing the stench. Ruben's body had been torn apart, limbs and organs were thrown everywhere. It was a gruesome and horrible end for a good man. Christy shined the light onto some of the limbs and they were covered with teeth and claw marks. “She’s an animal, a cruel disgusting animal.” Christy said with anger in her voice.

“That and maybe she did this on purpose. For us to see and hopefully scare us away. She may be an animal but she’s smart, she knew that we would come looking for her. She knew that I would do whatever I had to in order to find her and try to stop her. She's probably listening to us as we make our way down the rabbit hole.” Chuck was looking around as he was speaking to Christy.

He threw his glowstick a few feet ahead of them and watched it roll further down into the darkness. He looked at Christy as she cracked another one and handed it to him. They continued in the direction that he threw the glowstick. After about another ten feet they stopped when they heard a noise, it sounded like someone had kicked a rock down the corridor. Then they heard a faint laugh, she was there.

“Start cracking all the glowsticks.” Chuck whispered to Christy.

She began cracking them and passing each one to him. Chuck was throwing the glowsticks all around the chamber they had just entered. Each one gave off a haunting eerie green glow and they were lighting the area just enough that they could see her crawling down the cave wall about twenty feet away from them. Christy aimed the beam of light from the flashlight directly at her.

The woman, who was barely that, looked to be in her early to mid twenties. She had golden blonde hair and piercing eyes that reflected the light of the flashlight like a mirror. As she moved closer to them her nails began to extend and she bared her pointed teeth with an evil hiss.

"Don't look into her eyes." Chuck told Christy as she immediately looked to the floor.

"Good memory." The woman told Chuck. "Do you remember anything else about her?"

There was something familiar about her but Chuck wasn't quite sure what it was. He saw something in her eyes before he had looked away to warn Christy. "I remember plenty. I remember the day Charles met her, how it was after he found that town that she massacred. I remember that she attacked Jacob all because she believed Charles was replacing Chloe, when all he was doing was honoring a promise that he made to his dying friend. I remember how Cassandra blamed herself for Chloe's death and she made Charles believe that she was gone forever." Chuck grabbed the object that had fallen from his suitcase and threw it in front of the woman. It was Chloe's doll and if he was right, it was her doll.

She knelt down and picked it up. She looked at it fondly and then threw it into the darkness. "Is that supposed to change anything?" She charged at them, hitting Chuck so hard that he flew into Christy and she hit the wall behind them.

Her head bounced off of the wall and she hit the ground with a heavy thud. Chuck quickly ran over to her, calling her name. "Christy. Christy, are you ok? PLease wake up." He shook her but she did not open her eyes. He could feel a pulse and her breathing.

"Chloe, why are you doing this? Cassandra never said anything about you coming back after they buried you. Charles loved you more than anything in this world. Please stop this." Chuck pleaded with Chloe.

"His Chloe died with her mother. The mother he murdered and replaced with some pathetic human bitch. A woman I was happy to kill in my mothers name. Just like I did Jacob. He plotted with Charles and you, so I removed his head to stop his plotting thoughts. And you, you're nothing but a cheap imitation of the man who murdered my mother. I was able to manipulate you so easily. I made you believe she was alive and wanted you to join her. Just like she did with my father. I wanted you to know what she felt for him and all that she was prepared to give him, except I always planned to rip everything away from you." She glared at him and swung her clawed hand at his face.

He was able to avoid her first swing but did not see the second one coming. She scratched the left side of his face and he let out a painful yell. He gripped the axe with both hands and swung it at her. Each swing missed her as she moved with incredible speed. She grabbed the axe from him after a failed wild swing and she threw it across the chamber of the cave. She grabbed chuck by the back of his shirt and flung him across the room, he fell to the ground gasping for air.

Christy was starting to stir, she opened her eyes just in time to see Chloe throw Chuck and then jump on top of her. She reached for the flashlight and hit Chloe across the face. Chloe's head barely turned and she was back to glaring at her. Christy shouted for Chuck but she couldn't see him. She reached into her pocket and grabbed the one silver spoon that she was able to flatten at the cabin. She jammed it into Chloe's side and somehow it broke skin like a knife.

Chloe screamed in pain. She reached for Christy's hand and began squeezing it while she still had a grip on the spoon. She looked down at Christy with an evil smile. "Now it's your turn to scream." Chloe said to her as she tightened her grip so hard that she heard a loud "POP". It was the sound of one of Christy's fingers breaking.

Christy's scream was so loud that it was enough to make Chuck jump to his feet and run full speed at Chloe. He tackled her to the ground and grabbed one of the stakes that he carved. With both hands gripping the stake he brought it down as fast as he could, the stake pierced her flesh but it went through her left shoulder.

Chloe screamed in complete agony, she pushed Chuck away from her and she ran into the dark. "You son of a bitch, you will pay for that. You both will pay with your lives and when I am done with you, your friends will be next. After them I will go to each of your homes and slaughter every single family member I can find." She screamed at them.

Chuck stumbled over to Christy. “Can you stand and walk?”

“Yes.” She looked at him wondering what he was thinking.

“You need to go.” He said to her quietly. “I will distract her and you get out of here. Let me finish this myself.”

Christy looked at him in disbelief. “Are you out of your damn mind? I told you over and over, we are in this together.” Christy looked on in horror as Chuck's face cringed in pain.

Chloe had run up behind Chuck and jammed her clawed hand into his right side. She felt the warmth of his blood trickling down her hand. As she was about to bury her other hand into his back, he collapsed to the floor. She watched him drop like a sack of potatoes and smiled. Her smile disappeared as she felt something ripping into her chest.

Christy had grabbed the stake that killed Cassandra from Chuck’s pocket as he stood there with Chloe’s nails in his side. She mouthed the word “FALL” to him and he did as she said. As he collapsed to the ground, she saw what she had hoped, Chloe watching him hit the floor. With only seconds to react Christy plunged the stake into Chloe's chest. It ripped through her shirt, pierced her flesh and as if guided by an unseen force it went straight through her heart.

Chloe flew across the room landing on the wall of the cave. It was like something was holding her there in place as she screamed and thrashed around violently. Chloe's body began to burn, the chamber of the cave lit up as if the sun had risen inside of it. The flames got brighter and hotter with each passing second. Still planted to the cave wall Chloe let out one last final scream and then silence.

Christy grabbed Chuck's arms and helped him to his feet. "Now we can go."

Chuck chuckled for a second. "Wait." He grabbed the flashlight from the cave floor and aimed it at where Chloe's skeleton had become fused with the cave wall. He just stared at it for a moment. "Good-bye Chloe."

They made their way to the entrance of the cave, stumbling and tripping the entire way up. Once they got outside they collapsed to the sand and took in a big breath of fresh air. They just laid there for a moment. They could hear the waves crashing on to the shore, the seagulls squawking and it was peaceful. They looked at each other and smiled.

"Umm… I think we need to get to the hospital." Chuck said, as he was still wincing in pain.

"Oh shit. I forgot about Steven and Gloria." Christy replied.

Chuck looked at her baffled. "To hell with them, I'm bleeding from my side and your damn hand is broken."

Christy started laughing. "Oh yeah. OK let's go." She said groaning in pain as she stood up and then helped Chuck up.

They got to the van and Chuck drove them to the hospital. The moment they arrived at the ER, Chuck collapsed to the floor. The doctors and nurses ran over to him and rushed him away. Christy had her hand checked out, reset and casted. She went looking for Steven and Gloria while Chuck was being attended to. She stopped at the nurses station and asked where she could find her friends. The nurse walked her over to their room.

“Hey guys.” Christy said softly.

Steven smiled and Gloria ran over to Christy throwing her bandaged arms around her. They both cried for a moment and just held each other. Steven sat there just watching them.

“Are you two done?” He asked the sobbing friends. “Where is my cousin? Is he ok?” Steven said showing concern for Chuck.

“Oh sorry, he umm.. he was hurt and they had to rush him into surgery. I am waiting to hear an update.” Christy was wiping her tears away while talking to Steven.

Gloria looked at Christy with a stern and serious look. “Is this nightmare over?”

Just then the doctor walked in as the nurses rolled Chuck into the room across the hall. “OK. Who is here for the gentleman across the hall?”

Christy jumped up. “I am. Well, we all are here for him. Is he going to be ok?” She asked.

“We had to stitch up several penetrating wounds, he has two broken ribs and his shoulder was slightly dislocated. Overall, he will make a full recovery and he should be waking up soon. If I may ask, what happened?" The doctor asked curiously.

"He fell down a hole in one of the caves we were exploring." Christy said quickly.

"Hmm. I see. Well, in my personal and professional opinion, leave the cave exploring to the experts. I will be back to check on him this evening. We should be able to discharge all of you in the morning." The doctor left the room shaking his head.

When the morning came the four friends were discharged. They went back to the cabin and sat for a moment. They looked around and remained silent. None of them felt comfortable in the cabin or even on the island. Plus, none of them had any idea how they were going to explain Harper's disappearance. The silence was painful and unbearable.

"I think we should check out and just go home." Chuck said.

They all agreed at the same time. After that they packed up their stuff and Harpers, checked out of the hotel and got a taxi to the airport. They chose to pay extra to fly directly back home. They didn't want to sit through another long road trip. Chuck paid the extra amount for them to fly all the way back home, he felt guilty and it was the very least he could do. They all slept through the entire plane ride back.

"If we go on any other vacations, I am not picking a damn thing." Said Chuck to the group.

Steven and Gloria got into Stevens car, waved to them and left. Gloria would have to tell her parents that Harper fell ill on the island and passed from some dangerous disease. The body was cremated and that was why there was nothing to bury, but they would plant a headstone for her and have a memorial in her honor.

Chuck and Christy went back to his apartment. They sat there on the couch quietly mourning for Harper and Jacob. Two innocent people caught in the middle of a fight that had nothing to do with them but stole their lives from them. Chuck got up and walked over to the bedroom, Christy followed him. He changed his clothes and sat on the edge of the bed. Christy stepped into the bathroom, changed into some PJs and climbed into his bed. Chuck smiled at her, moved back and laid down next to her.

He was afraid to fall asleep. What if they missed something? What if she somehow survived? His mind was racing until Christy placed her head on his chest. She seemed to be able to silence his mind and slow it down. He hugged her tightly and drifted off to sleep.

Chuck opened his eyes and began to panic. There he was back on that same beach. He quickly started walking over to the fire pit because he saw someone sitting there with their back to him. He slowed down as he approached the person sitting and he saw it was a woman. He heard a voice say, “Hi handsome.” He smiled and stepped in front of the woman. It was Christy. She handed him a beer and he sat next to her. He pulled her closer to him and he kissed her. He looked her in the eyes and said, “Now this is a dream I can’t wait to enjoy.”

Epilogue

Steven and Gloria

After they arrived home, Steven went with Gloria to her parents house. He knew that having to tell her family about Harper was going to be one of, if not the most, difficult things she would ever have to do. They had taken an Uber from the airport back to his place and then he drove her home. The drive to her parents house, the place that the girls grew up in, was filled with emptiness. They didn't speak, turn on the radio or even answer the phone when Christy called them. All Steven could do was hold her hand.

As they pulled up to the house Gloria began to cry. She turned away from Steven as if she was trying to hide the tears. When she finally looked at him, he was wiping his own tears. Steven got out of the vehicle first. He walked over to her door, opened it and helped her out of the passenger seat. He pulled her close to him and he just held her. She buried her face in his chest and just sobbed for a moment. She stepped back and tried to dry her face but the tears just kept on rolling down her reddened face.

“Thank you for doing this with me Steve. I know you didn't have to but it means a lot that you are here with me.” She said to him as her lip quivered.

“There's no way I would let you do this by yourself. I still don't even believe what happened myself. Every time I close my eyes…” He had to stop to gather himself and keep the tears at bay.

“I know. Me too.” She said, grabbing his hand. “I guess we should go in and tell my parents.” She said with dread and heartache in her voice.

“Before we go in, what exactly are we going to tell them? We can't tell them the truth, they'll either think it's some sort of sick joke or they'll have us thrown into a looney bin.” Said Stevem with concern and confusion in his voice.

“We will tell them that Harper got incredibly sick while we were on the island. She died after contracting some deadly disease that the doctors fought to treat. The body was cremated to avoid whatever she had from spreading and causing some sort of pandemic. That is why there is no body to bury but they will send the ashes once they're certain that there is no chance of the disease spreading.” She stopped to take a breath and look at him.

"That is what we will tell them and that is what we will have to stick with for the rest of our lives."

He looked at her in shock. "How did you come up with all that so fast?" He asked.

"It's partly true, if you think about it, but I was trying to figure it out during the flight and the drive here." She said as she tried to make herself believe that the story was what really happened.

"Wow. Ok. Are you ready?" He asked her, as he grabbed her hand.

"No but what choice do we have?" She said feeling exhausted.

They both took a deep breath and made their way to the front door. Gloria grabbed her keys out of her purse and opened the door. They stepped inside and walked to the kitchen where they could hear her parents talking to each other. The moment they walked through the kitchen doorway Gloria broke down into tears.

"Sweetie, what's wrong?" Her mother, Mary, said as she ran over to Gloria to try and calm her.

"Gloria, talk to us baby. Why are you crying? Steven, what's going on?" Her father, Jeff, asked them.

Steven with tears in his eyes looked at Gloria and then at her parents. He told them the fictional story about what happened. When he finished he just stood there as both of Gloria's parents stared at him in disbelief.

In full denial Jeff yelled at Steven, “You’re lying. Why would you make up such a crazy story about Harper? Where is she? This has to be a cruel and despicable joke. Where is my baby girl?” As he stepped towards Steven his knees buckled and he began to fall to the floor.

Steven ran over to him and caught him before he hit the floor. As Steven helped Jeff back to his feet, he pushed Steven away. Her father stood there glaring at Steven and was about to move towards him again.

“Daddy stop. He's telling the truth. I was supposed to be the one to tell you and mom but I just couldn't get the words out.” Gloria began crying again but was still able to speak. “Steve was there with me the whole time, he never left mine and Harper's side.”

Steven looked at her father and mother with tears pouring out of his eyes. “I am so sorry.” Those were the only words left that he could find to say.

Gloria's father walked over to Steven and put his hand on his shoulder. He looked Steven in the eyes, pulled him closer and hugged him. Even as he began to cry he kept hugging Steven. “Thank you for that. You're a good man Steven and Gloria is lucky to have someone like you.”

His words cut Steven like a hot knife through butter. Even his hand, when he placed it on Steven's shoulder, felt so incredibly heavy. He knew that he had to keep the facade going so he forced a half smile and thanked him. Her mother walked over to him and hugged him as well.

Gloria's father moved past Steven and went straight to Gloria. They both cried and he just held on to her. Mary joined them and they just stood there crying together as a broken family.

Gloria was the first one to break away from their arms and she walked over to Steven. She looked at him, with tear filled eyes and thanked him for stepping in for her. She kissed him on the cheek and hugged him tighter than she had ever hugged anyone. “Thank you Steve. Thank you so very much.” She gave him a small smile.

“When will they send her ashes home sweetie?” Her father asked.

“They need to make sure that there is absolutely no chance of any type of possible contagion remaining. They said it would be maybe a month, two at the most.” Gloria said, trying to keep herself from crying again.

“Do they know what she had or how she got it?” Her father asked.

"No. It moved through her system so fast that they weren't able to diagnose her. They were pretty sure it wasn't contagious, since none of us got sick but they didn't want to take any chances with whatever it was." She was adding extra details to make the story more believable and to hopefully stop them from asking any more questions.

Mary and Jeff walked over to the dining room table and sat down. They remained there, quietly trying to process the horrific news that had just dropped on them. The look on their faces was of complete devastation and heartbreak. Jeff grabbed Mary's hand as she began crying. Quiet tears turned into uncomfortable sobs in an instant. Jeff himself was crying but his face was void of emotion. He looked numb and shattered.

Gloria grabbed Stevens hand and walked with him to the table. She sat down and Steven stood behind her with his hands gently resting on her shoulders. Gloria was already grieving the loss of her twin sister but now guilt was added to her pain. She could see that her parents were heart broken and she knew that, in part, she was responsible for it. Granted she had absolutely no control over the events that led to her sister's terrible death, lying to her parents made that wound so much deeper.

Steven leaned forward and spoke quietly into Gloria's ear. “Maybe we should go? You can stay at my place if it's too much being back here.” Steven was worried about Gloria and he had no idea how she would be able to rest in the house that her and Harper grew up in.

Gloria looked up at him, with tear filled eyes. “I…I want to stay.” She responded to him.

“Please, stay. We would appreciate it if you both would stay. Steven, you can stay in the spare room, if you'd like.” Mary looked at them with hopes that they would both agree to remain at the house.

Steven reluctantly agreed to stay in the spare room. “Yeah, sure. Of course we'll stay the night. Is there anything I can do for anyone? If you're hungry, I can order something.” Steven said as he forced a smile.

“Don't be silly. We can take care of that. How about we order a pizza?” Mary said as she tried to control the tears falling down her face.

Jeff stood up and walked over to the fridge. He grabbed four cans of Pepsi and set them on the table in front of each of them. He grabbed his phone, ordered 2 large pizzas and paid for them over the phone. “They said they'll be here in about forty-five minutes. If you'll excuse me, I need to use the bathroom." Jeff said in a soft monotone voice.

Steven sat down next to Gloria, wondering if he was going to be able to get any sleep at all. He watched Mary get up from the table and walk over to the closet down the hall. She came back with several photo albums and placed them on the table. He quietly sighed because he knew it was going to be a night of reminiscing and old stories.

Mary opened one of the albums after Jeff returned from the bathroom. It was filled with baby pictures of the girls and holidays that they celebrated as babies. She would pass pictures around the table and cry a bit with each photo. This went on until the pizza arrived and continued after they ate, which wasn't very much. They each had maybe a slice or two of pizza and nothing more. The closed boxes became cluttered with old photos.

After about two hours of passing photos, Jeff stood up and put the pizza boxes in the fridge. "I think we are going to call it a night." He said with that same monotone voice. He helped Mary out of her chair and they both walked to the side of the table where Gloria and Steven sat. They hugged them both tightly, said goodnight and went upstairs to their room.

Steven sat there for a moment longer and looked up at Gloria. She was sitting still, no expression on her face and not moving a muscle. She was like a stake. He placed a hand on her shoulder and she jumped. “Sorry, I didn't mean to startle you. Do you want to go lay down?” He asked her.

“Yeah, I think I do. I am so tired. I feel like I am mentally and physically drained. This was the worst night of my life and I really want this day to be over. You know what I mean.” She said to him, as she looked at the floor.

“Yeah. I do Glo. I really do. Come on, I'll walk you to your room.” He said with a hand stretched out for her to grab onto.

“Thank you Steve. Thank you so much.” She grabbed his hand to stand up and then moved closer towards him. She kissed him and hugged him. “I wouldn't have been able to do this or handle telling my parents without you.” She said with her head resting on his chest.

“I'm here for you Glo.” He whispered back to her as he rested his head on top of hers.

They walked upstairs to her and Harper's room. Standing outside at the door for a moment, Gloria took a deep breath and opened the door. They had always shared a room, even when their parents offered to let one of them take the spare room, they chose to stay together.

Each side was decorated in a way that perfectly matched that sister's personality. They each had their own trophies, Harper's were for softball and Gloria's were for soccer. They had the same taste in music and movies so there were shared posters of boy bands and movie characters. Harper was a bit messier than Gloria and it showed with her bed covers crumpled up on the side of the bed. Gloria's bed was neatly made, decorated with throw pillows and a blanket with cats all over it.

Gloria walked over to Harper's bed and picked up one of her pillows. She walked over to her bed and laid there hugging Harper's pillow. She began crying and she buried her face into the pillow.

Steven walked over to her, sat on the edge of the bed and gently rubbed her back as she cried. “I'm so sorry Glo.” It was the only thing he could think to say to her.

“I know.” She said sniffling. “You can go ahead to the spare room. I'll be ok. I love you Steve.” She said, trying to give him a smile.

"I love you too, Glo. If you need me, I'm not far. Just text or call me and I'll come right over.” He leaned down and kissed her head.

Steven went over to the spare room which was two doors down from where Gloria's room was. Her parents room was down the opposite end of the hallway. Through the doors and space of the hallway, he could hear her parents crying and talking in their room. He walked into the room and sat down on the bed. He pulled out his phone and began scrolling through his own collection of photos, both new and older ones. He stopped on the picture they took of all of them before they left for the island vacation.

The smiles and excitement on their faces reminded him of when their only worry was who was going to drive and where they were going to stop for food. As he looked at the photo he began to feel angry towards his cousin. He wondered, how much did Chuck know about what was going to happen? Did he know that they were going to be in that kind of danger? How much of it was he hiding and how much of it was Christy aware of? His phone faded and the screen went blank for a moment.

He clicked the power button and went to his text messages. He glared at Chuck's name and wanted to text him, asking him all the questions that were burning in his mind. He even pressed on Chuck's name and looked at the keyboard, debating whether he should ask him or not. He decided against it for the moment and put his phone down next to the pillow. Steven landed his head on the pillow and turned off the lights.

Steven tossed and turned for at least an hour. Every time he closed his eyes he would see Harper screaming in the sand as her body erupted in flames. His eyes shot open and he stared at the emptiness of the ceiling. Eventually he fell back asleep and thankfully he didn't dream of the horrid events. However, his mind went back to that day when he thought he saw Chuck's reflection standing while Chuck collapsed to the floor of the gas station bathroom. He remembered Chuck asking him not to mention it to anyone and then when he was someone standing behind the rental as they were leaving the store.

Steven opened his eyes and it was now morning. He sat up on the edge of the bed and yawned. He was dreading going downstairs to face Mary and Jeff again. He walked over to the bathroom, peed and threw some cold water on his face. After drying off he walked over to the girls room, he found Gloria sitting on her bed looking at her phone. He walked in and sat down next to her.

"Did you get any sleep?" He asked while yawning again.

"Some. Not a whole lot. Every time I closed my eyes I kept seeing her. One time, I sat up and I could have sworn she was laying in her bed. I ran over to her bed thinking maybe the whole island trip was just a nightmare but the bed was empty. I slept for about another hour and then I was awake. So, I just sat here. I wrote something for her that I'll read when we have a funeral or memorial for her." Gloria said with a crack in voice. "Did you get any rest?"

Steven replied, "I slept on and off but it was not restful. Before I fell asleep I started getting angry at Chuck, wondering so many things about how much of what happened could have been avoided if we had just listened to him. I was about to text him but decided to try to sleep instead."

"There is plenty of blame to go around. Even if we had listened to his crazy stories, would we have actually believed him or would we have checked him into a hospital and gone to the island without him? Then would we have all been killed or turned into what it was that was hunting us. Did going there with him save the rest of us? There are a lot of what ifs and scenarios that who knows what could have happened or gone differently." She wasn't exactly sticking up for Chuck but she knew that he wasn't the only one to blame for what happened.

"Wow. I mean yeah, you're right. I didn't think about all that. Damn." He said feeling guilty about putting all the blame on his cousin. "Do you want to get out of here? Maybe go grab some breakfast or we can just go to my place and try to rest." He asked her.

"Let me check on my parents first. Then yeah, I could use some breakfast and more sleep." She said while smiling at him.

Gloria got off her bed and made her way down to her parents bedroom. She knocked softly on the door and slowly opened the door. She could see them sleeping in bed still and they had pictures all over the bed and floor. Her mom had fallen asleep holding an old photo from their first Christmas. She quietly closed the door and went back to her room to let Steven know that they were still sleeping.

"I just need to use the bathroom and then we can go. Ok?" She said as she kissed him on the cheek.

Steven nodded and waited there for her to go to the bathroom and come back. It was only a few minutes and she was back. She grabbed his hand and they headed out to the SUV. Steven opened her door for her to get in and closed it once she was inside. He went around to the driver's side, climbed in and started the explorer up. He began driving towards a restaurant so they could get some breakfast.

After they finished their food, Steven drove them back to his place. They walked inside, went straight to the bedroom, laid down and fell asleep instantly in each other's arms. Neither of them had any bad dreams and they slept for a solid four hours.

Steven woke up to the sound of his phone buzzing. He looked at the screen and saw that it was Chuck calling him. He watched the phone ring for a few seconds then he hit the volume button, silencing the buzzing and fell back asleep with Gloria in his arms.

They both woke up around seven o'clock. They looked at each other and smiled. Gloria leaned over and kissed Steven, then got up to use the bathroom. She came back with a surprised look on her face and looked at Steven.

"Whats wrong?" He asked her.

"I have like eight missed calls and twelve text messages, all from Chuck and Christy. Mostly just them checking on us and somehow Chuck found someone to get a legal death certificate for Harper. That way we can officially bury her and no one will suspect anything from any of us." She looked up at Steven with genuine surprise.

"I wonder how he was able to do that." Steven said as he looked at his own phone. "Thats cool of him to figure that out for her. He messaged me about the same thing and he apologized for everything that happened on the island.

He said he feels responsible and awful about all of it. He said that he will pay for the headstone for her memorial." Steven looked up at Gloria who was standing there crying and smiling at the same time.

About three weeks had gone by and Gloria received a call from a funeral home that the headstone was finally ready. She called her parents to let them know about the headstone being ready. She text Steven to let him know about it as well. She text Chuck thanking him again for paying for the headstone and that it was ready for them to set up her memorial.

The following week was the first time since the island that Steven and Gloria had seen Chuck and Christy. It was a somber reunion but was met with hugs and kind words. Steven initially had a hard time looking at his cousin but once Chuck approached him, they hugged like they hadn't seen each other in decades. Christy and Gloria started crying the moment they saw each other and continued crying as they embraced.

Chuck and Christy walked up to Jeff and Mary and hugged them both. "We are so sorry for your loss. Harper was a great girl and she was an amazing friend. We both miss her so much and we think about her all the time." Chuck spoke for himself and Christy, who was still crying.

“Thank you for your kind words Chuck. I know Harper cared a great deal for the both of you and I know she would be happy that you both are here for her and for Gloria.” Jeff said to them.

More people slowly arrived for the memorial for Harper. There were friends from school, people she worked with and family. They all made their way to Jeff, Mary and Gloria to extend their condolences and sympathies. There was even a well dressed gentleman who claimed to have been a manager of hers from a former job that she had worked at but no one recognized him.

The time came to finally begin the memorial. Jeff was the one to start the event.

“I'd like to thank everyone for coming and showing support for my family. Harper was an amazing daughter, a wonderful sister and as we can see a great friend. It warms my heart to see all of you here.” Jeff paused for a moment to gather himself as his emotions were trying to get the best of him. “As you all know Harper's passing was unexpected and extremely tragic. I am grateful that her sister and her friends were around her when she left. We will forever miss her and we will keep her in our hearts. Thank you again.” Jeff stepped away to let the family priest begin with some prayers and memories he had of Harper.

Once the priest was done, Gloria walked up to the headstone and placed her hand on it. She turned to face the crowd of people who were there to celebrate her sister's life. "Thank you all for coming today. Seeing all of you here reminds me of the type of person my sister was. She was always so kind and considerate of others, always willing to help anyone in need, and she had the biggest heart that was full of love. I wrote something for her, I know how much she liked to write so I thought it would be a good way to help say my goodbyes to her." Gloria had begun crying, Steven went up to her, hugged her and held her for a moment. "I'm sorry. Ok. Here it is.

I think about you everyday
Even more on this very day
I miss you
And I love you
All the fun times we had
And you're not here which makes me sad
I cried that day I said goodbye
But I smile every time I look up to the sky
I know you're looking down watching me grow
My memories of you pick me up when I am low
I know you're in a better place
And that thought keeps the smile on my face

Today is your day
And it's a very somber day
I wish you were here to hug and to kiss
Our times together I surely do miss
I know one day we'll be together
And on that day there will be beautiful weather
Sunny smiles and clear eyes
Winded talks and some melting Hi's
So even though we are far apart
You will forever and always remain in my heart.

I miss you so much and I love you Harper." She set the poem down on top of the headstone and with Steven at her side she walked over to her parents.

Jeff and Mary both hugged Gloria and thanked her for writing something so beautiful for Harper. They walked up to the headstone and turned to face everyone. "Thank you all again for coming out today. We appreciate it so much. I know Harper is looking down on us all right now and smiling at the show of love you have all given her. I hope you all get home safe and please tell those you love how much you love and appreciate them. We never know how much time we have on this earth and any moment could be our last. We love you all." Jeff said with Mary at his side.

Everyone began to make their way to their vehicles except for Gloria, Steven, Christy and Chuck. They stood there in silence for a moment longer. In the distance, Chuck could see the stranger who claimed to have worked with Harper, he was just standing there watching them. Christy noticed Chuck's unsettling stare and decided to speak first before he could say anything about him.

"That poem you wrote was beautiful Gloria, Harper would have loved it. The whole ceremony was really beautiful." Said Christy.

"Yes, such a great turn out and your poem was amazing." Chuck added to Christy's comment.

"Thank you both. It wouldn't have been possible without you guys. I mean we would have had a memorial but it might have been a few months later instead of today." Said Gloria to Chuck and Christy.

Steven had seen that Chuck kept glancing over at someone standing off to their side. "Everything OK Cuz?" Steven asked him.

"Does anyone know that guy?" Chuck asked the group.

They all responded "No" in unison.

"He seems a bit odd just standing there." Christy said. "Do you guys want to grab a bite to eat?" She asked.

“I'm not very hungry. Haven't really had much of an appetite lately. I know it'll get easier with time but I kinda just want to go lay down.” Gloria said as she held on to Stevens arm.

“Maybe another time then. We are here for you guys if you need anything.” Chuck said to Steven and Gloria.

“We know cuz and we appreciate it. Today was just a lot to deal with. We're gonna get going but I'll text ya later.” Steven said as he hugged Chuck.

They all hugged each other and said their goodbyes.

They drove behind Chuck until they got to the gate of the cemetery. Steven waved to them as he turned left on the street, Chuck waved back and turned right. They watched each other as they drove away in their rearview mirrors until both cars were gone and out of sight. Steven looked over at Gloria, smiled at her and grabbed her hand.

“I'm not ready for that just yet.” Steven said to Gloria as they drove back to his place.

“I would like to see them soon. Maybe we can try for something next week. We can't avoid them for Steve. They are our friends and Chuck is your family.” Gloria said, trying to be sympathetic to his feelings.

"I know babe. Ok, next week. If you wanna set something up I'll make it work." He said while keeping his focus on the road. He could see her watching his facial expressions, so he smiled at her. "I promise Glo. I will make it work and show up."

"Ok. I'll text Christy now. We can do something chill like dinner." Gloria said with excitement in her voice.

Steven was glad to hear her getting happy about something. It had been a while since he heard something other than sadness from her. He glimpsed over at her and smiled as he watched her typing away. He knew it wasn't really Chuck's fault but part of him was having a hard time fully forgiving him. Even Gloria was able to find a way to not place the blame on him. Maybe this dinner would be the stepping he needed to move past those feelings.

Steven felt a bit of relief when they got back to his place. They had been staying at Gloria's parents house ever since they got back. It seemed like forever since he had been home. He missed the way it felt, plus, there was a certain level of comfort that he was needing and being there was filling that. He had been there a couple times to pick up the mail and grab some clothes to wear. As he sat on his bed and laid back, he let out a loud relaxing sigh.

Gloria laughed. "Wow, that good huh?"

“So good.” He chuckled. “Come over here and lay down with me.” Steven said to her.

“I'm not tired, maybe later.” She replied to him.

“I'm not tired either but just come lay down with me for a second. Then we'll get up and order some food.” Steven said to Gloria.

"You had me at food.” Gloria said while laughing as she made her way over to him. She climbed onto the bed next to him and laid next to him with her head on his shoulder. “Ok, I get it now.”

They just laid there for about 30 minutes. Not moving or saying anything at all. Steven was the first to move when he reached for his phone. He looked at the screen and saw he had a couple of notifications. One was an email from the bank and the other was a missed call from an unknown number. He swiped both away, hit the search bar and looked up the number for the Italian restaurant down the street from his place. He ordered himself a large spaghetti and meatballs, and for Gloria a large fettuccine alfredo with grilled chicken. He paid and set his phone back down.

Gloria got up to use the restroom and went over to his nightstand to grab his remote. She turned on the tv and went straight to amazon prime. She browsed the movies for a bit and landed on one of her and Harper's favorite movies, *The Little Shop of Horrors.* They had probably seen the movie about fifty times and the play about ten times. She smiled as she hit play and set the remote down on the nightstand next to the side of the bed she was on.

"Hey, there was something that bothered me today at the memorial." Gloria said as she rolled to her side to face Steven. "That guy that said he was a manager for a place that Harper used to work at."

"Yeah, I remember who you're talking about." Steven replied.

"We both worked at all of the same places and I have never seen him before. There may have been like maybe one job that we both didn't work at but the manager was also the owner and my dad knew him. I'm pretty certain that he was lying about who he was or who he was pretending to be." Gloria said with a hint of paranoia in her voice.

"That is pretty weird. There was definitely something off about him but I couldn't put my finger on it. Even Chuck commented on how strange the guy seemed as he was standing there watching us." Steven was interrupted by the sound of someone knocking on the door.

Gloria jumped and looked at the door with a scared look in her eyes. She quickly looked at Steven who was already making his way towards the door. “Be careful Steve.” She whispered loudly to him.

He looked back and smiled, “No worries babe. It's just the delivery person with our food.” He said calmly. Though as he turned to continue towards the front door his calmness was replaced with hesitation and nervousness. As he got to the door he slowly looked through the peephole on the door. At first he didn't see anyone but then a figure stood up with his back to the door.

“Hello?” Said the person outside of the door as he turned around and knocked again.

“One sec.” Steven laughed in relief. It was just the food, like he had said to Gloria. He opened the door, paid the delivery guy and brought the food in. He placed the food on the table in his dining room and called for Gloria. “Babe, dinner is ready.”

“Ok. Let me pause the movie.” She joined Steven at the table but looked at him with confusion. There was a second to-go container on top of her food. “What's this? I can smell the alfredo sauce but what else did you order?” She asked him.

He smiled, “Just a little appetizer I picked out for ya, open it.” Steven has begun to slowly walk to her side of the table.

“Ok.” She replied excitedly. As she opened the container, she noticed Steven walking towards her. She looked down at the open container then looked at Steven and again at the container. There was a small, blue cube shaped box inside of the to-go container.

Steven grabbed the smaller box and dropped down to one knee as he opened it. “Gloria, we have been through a lot lately and it has made me realize a few things. 1. You never know how long we really have in this life. 2. We are strong together and I have never felt closer to anyone like I do with you. 3. I can't imagine my life without you in it and I want to spend the rest of our lives together. I love you Glo. I love you so much and I want to spend everyday for the rest of my life showing you how much I love you. Gloria, will you marry me?” He knelt there nervously awaiting her answer.

Her eyes had welled up with tears, she looked at the shining ring in the box he held and she said yes. “Yes Steven, of course I will. You have stood by me, with me, after all that has happened and all that we have seen. You mean the world to me and I love you so much.” She wiped her tears with the one hand she had free as Steven slid the ring on her other hand.

She hugged him so tight and kissed him repeatedly. “I need to call my parents and tell them. I need to call Christy and tell her. I'm so happy.” She said smiling ear to ear.

“Your parents already know, they're just waiting for a call to find out your answer.” He smiled as he opened her food container. “Don't forget to eat your dinner.” He said laughing.

Gloria called her parents to give them the good news as she and Steven ate their dinner. They were so happy to hear the good news and congratulated them. Her mom made it very clear that she wanted to help with anything and everything Gloria needed. Her father said that it would be his honor and mean so much to him if they let them pay for the wedding. Gloria then called Christy to tell her the news and asked her to be her Maid of Honor. She accepted and said congrats to the two of them.

Steven called his parents and told them the good news, they were so happy for the two of them. He texted Chuck about the good news and said he was looking forward to seeing them next week. Chuck texted him back congratulations and he couldn't wait to see them and celebrate the great news. Steven put the phone down, went over to his new fiance and hugged her so tight.

After talking about wedding dates for the better part of a week, they finally decided to set the date. May 22nd, 2027, which was roughly years away, would be the day that they would get married. That would give them ample time to plan, prepare and get everything reserved for the big day.

Steven immediately said, "No island honeymoons, let's do a cruise instead." He was serious and trying to smile when he said it.

Gloria agreed. "How about a Disney cruise?" She suggested, since she had never been to Disney or on a cruise.

"Ok. That sounds great, babe." Steven chuckled and smiled at her.

They walked over to the couch and sat down. Steven grabbed the remote and put on the movie, *Edward Scissorhands.* It was one of their favorites. Gloria brought over some popcorn and they cuddled up on the couch. "I can't wait til we do this as husband and wife," Steven said as he grabbed a handful of popcorn.

"Me too babe." Gloria said as she rested her head on his shoulder. "Me too."

Chuck and Christy

As soon as Chuck and Christy stepped off of the plane, they all felt a bitter moment of relief. Relief was replaced by guilt and sadness because they had lost people on what should have been a fun filled vacation. Even though Christy didn't know Jacob, she could feel the heartache that was lingering in Chuck. This only added to the pain they already felt over Harper. Feeling relief just seemed wrong to them but they had to be grateful that they were still alive.

Regardless of the fact that Chuck was ready to sacrifice his life if that was what it took, losing Jacob and Harper was devastating. Harper he had known for years, her and Gloria were like sisters to him. He felt so much guilt over her death that it was making him physically ill. His stomach was in knots, he had no appetite and every so often he caught himself shedding tears for his stolen sister. Jacobs' death was a complicated one for him. He had only really known him for a short while, but with Charles's memories it seemed as if he had known him forever. He knew that Jacob's life, both times, had ended too soon.

What really hit Chuck hard was the way that he died, now and in the past. It was brutal, hateful and so incredibly unfair.

For Christy losing Harper hurt her heart so much. She was such a sweet, loving and amazing friend. They had known each other for so long that the idea of her being dead was difficult for her to grasp. She wished the whole trip was just a terrible, horrible nightmare. She kept waiting to wake up, with a hangover instead of heartbreak, and see Harper there laughing at the crazy night they had all taken part in. Unfortunately, as much as Christy wanted to deny it, it was no nightmare. Monsters really do exist and they had come face to face with one. She felt bad for Chuck for his grief over Jacob, but for her the pain of losing Harper was far greater.

"Christy, I need to do something for Harper. I am going to call Steven and Gloria and tell them that I am going to pay for a headstone for her. She deserves at least that, a place where her family can go to say goodbye or visit her. I really need to do this." Chuck said with tears rolling down his face.

"I understand and I would like to help you pay for it, but you need to know that it's not your fault baby. I know you feel like it is but you can not take this blame all on yourself. This was Chloe, not you." Christy said to him as she hugged Chuck trying to comfort him.

"It really is my fault. I let us go to that island. I knew that someone or something was waiting for me there, granted I never thought it would be Chloe. But I could have stopped us from going. Even if it meant looking like a complete psycho and ending up in a psych hospital. I should have done something to stop that trip." Chuck had walked from Christy's hug to the couch in his living room and sat there with his head in his hands.

"Then it is both of our fault. I knew everything that you did and still went along with going there. I knew the truth and lied to make Harper believe we were just working through your nightmare. So, if you're going to take the blame for this, you better share that guilt with me because I am just as culpable." Christy was now sitting next to chuck and crying as well.

Chuck knew she was right but he didn't want to share any of that guilt or pain with her. He put her in that position. She may have known what was going on but it was only because he let her in and burdened her with this horrific knowledge. "You only knew what you did because I told you. So, I still believe the fault falls completely on me. But I know you, Christy, and you will say that you chose to help me. That it was your decision to do and say what you did to her and the others." Chuck replied and smirked a little bit as he looked at her.

She had a guilty smile because she he was right and he did know her well. She nodded in agreement and grabbed his hand. "We can't change the past but we can look to the future and do what we can to make it a better one. Let's try to get a hold of Gloria and Steven. I'm guessing they are her parents' house, maybe we can help them break the news to her parents. Just so they know they're not alone." said Christy.

They both picked up their phones and tried calling Steven and Gloria. They each called them several times but had no luck. Chuck began looking at headstone prices, designs, details and placements. He figured it would cost him around five grand and he was more than fine with that. Since it was getting late he ordered some food for him and Christy, though they hardly ate much of it. They had given up on trying to talk to Gloria and Steven for the night.

Chuck had a friend at the county coroner's office. It was someone he used to work with while he was in college. She was the elected coroner and had been for several years. He worked in the office during the night and helped her when she would get new cases. She was very thorough when it came to her investigations and he learned a great deal from her. He always felt like the office was haunted, especially since the morgue was right down the hall but she would tell him that there were no such things as ghosts. There was one time that he swore he saw someone walking the halls but when he went to go and check no one was there. There were even strange noises in the morgue at night but she would just say it the bodies releasing gas and death settling in. He messaged her about making a death certificate for Harper and initially she was reluctant. She wanted to know what happened and why he needed it. When he told her the short version of the story, leaving out the past memories he had gained, she told him that he needed to get some help. He insisted that the events really happened and reminded her that she technically owed him a favor. He had done some work on her car that would have cost her a few thousand dollars at a mechanics shop. She agreed but told him that she didn't like this idea. She said the certificate would be ready in a few days and he could pick it up when she received it. He thanked her repeatedly and told her he owed her this time because this was a huge favor.

Chuck sent a text to both Gloria and Steven then he went to sleep. "Hey guys, I just wanted to talk to you both and say how sorry I am about everything. I am so truly and incredibly sorry about Harper. I feel awful and I take full responsibility for what happened. Never in a million years did I think that anything like what happened could even be possible. That being said, I wanted to tell you both that I am going to pay for a headstone for Harper, she deserves a memorial and somewhere that people can say goodbye. Also, I know someone in the county coroner's office and I am getting a legal death certificate for Harper. I just wanted to tell you guys that and I hope we can get together soon and talk. I love you both." He hit send and went to sleep. Christy had already passed out while he was doing his research and messaging his friend at the coroner's office.

In the morning, he told Christy about the death certificate and his message to Steven and Gloria. She was amazed that he was able to get it and she was glad that he texted them. About thirty minutes later he got a reply from both of them thanking him for what he did and that they would let him and Christy know when the memorial was. They weren't quite ready for a get together but when they were they'd let him know. Chuck read the text to Christy.

"Thats understandable. I'm sure they'll come around soon enough." She said to him as he sat there looking a bit defeated. “It's a hard time for them, for all of us, but just give them some time.” Christy said.

“I know. I guess I was just hoping we would all be able to talk. But you're right, this is probably harder on them since they had to tell her parents.” Chuck agreed with Christy.

“Christy, I was wondering if maybe you wanted to move in with me? I love you and I have really enjoyed waking up with you here. I would like to make it a permanent thing, if you want to?” He sat there nervously waiting for her answer.

“I love you too and I would love that. The lease on my apartment is up this month too, so it's perfect timing.” She said, smiling at him.

“I kinda already made you a key. I was hoping you would say yes, to moving in. I can help you back up your apartment and get things moved in here.” He said as he walked over to her and kissed her.

It only took a few days to get everything packed up and moved over. She sold her old furniture and used the money to rent a moving truck. Their first night living together was so incredibly peaceful, they had the best night's sleep since before they left for that horrid vacation.

They even cooked dinner together and it was incredibly delicious. They fell asleep watching a movie in bed.

It had been about three weeks since they had paid for the headstone that Harper and Gloria's parents picked out. Gloria's parents had no idea that it was Chuck and Christy who paid for it. The funeral home just said that it was already taken care of and they didn't need to worry themselves with any payments. Chuck and Christy got a text from Gloria saying the headstone was ready. She told them that the memorial would be next Saturday and she hoped they would be able to attend. Chuck text her back saying that they would be at the memorial. Christy had responded to the message as well saying the same thing.

The week had gone by quickly and the day of the memorial was finally upon them.

"Is it weird that I am nervous about seeing Steven, Gloria and her parents." Chuck asked Christy as he buttoned up his shirt.

"No, I am nervous too. I am glad that we will be able to see them and that her parents will have some type of closure but at the same time the guilt is still there." Christy said to Chuck while she was sitting on the edge of the bed.

"That's exactly what I am feeling. I'm thankful that I have you here with me and that you understand how I'm feeling or how we are feeling." Chuck tried to smile but it was difficult for him.

His hands were shaking as he was trying to button the rest of his shirt. Christy walked over to him and hugged him. When she stepped back, she helped him with the last few buttons he had left. She grabbed his tie, slipped it around his neck and tied it for him. She looked up at him, smiled and walked over to the bathroom so she could finish getting ready.

Chuck sat down on the edge of the bed and put on his socks and shoes. He just sat there after he was finished and waited for Christy to finish getting ready. Once she was done, she walked out of the bathroom and he just stared at her.

"Wow. You look beautiful. Is that inappropriate since we are about to go to Harper's memorial?" Chuck said to Christy, who was smiling at him.

"If it were anybody other than us, it probably would be, but I'm sure Harper would expect nothing less from us." She replied to Chuck.

"You make a good point ma'am." He said as he moved closer to Christy and planted a kiss on her lips.

"I usually do," she replied laughing as she finished getting ready.

They left their apartment and drove to where Harper's memorial was being held. Chuck started getting a strange feeling as he drove through the cemetery, it was that same feeling he got when was in the dreams and Cassandra was watching him. Though, as he thought about it, it was probably Chloe that was watching him then. He felt a chill run up his spine as he looked around and past some of the headstones. It was an eerie and unsettling feeling but also very familiar.

"You ok? I've seen that look before." Christy asked Chuck. She could see the serious look on his face and the last time she saw that look was when they were heading to the island.

"Yeah I'm ok. I just had this weird feeling but it's probably just because being here for Harper's memorial is bringing back some scary feelings." Chuck said to her. He could tell that she was watching his facial expressions and could clearly see the look of paranoia that he had in his eyes.

"It's a lot to deal with and being here means that it really happened and Harper is really gone. The finality of it all is overwhelming and the realization that monsters are real is terrifying. We just need to focus on the fact that we survived, Gloria, Steven, you and me. We are still here and we need to live each day for her." Christy said as a tear rolled down her cheek.

"And for Jacob. I know we barely knew him but with Charles's memories, I feel like I've known him for years." Chuck gave her a half smile as he slowed the car down and parked behind Steven's Explorer.

She grabbed his hand and gave it a gentle squeeze. "For them both." Christy said to him with a smile.

Chuck smiled back at her and then got out of his vehicle. He walked over to the passenger side, opened the door for Christy and helped her out of the car. Christy put her arm around Chuck's as they began walking to Harper's headstone. They could see the gathering of her family and friends. Immediately they both walked up to her parents, expressed their sympathies and condolences. They went over to Steven and Gloria next, giving them both hugs and asking how they were holding up.

"It's been rough lately but not having to worry about the cost of the headstone was a huge relief and so very appreciated. You know, you didn't have to do that. When we told my folks that the cost was covered, they broke down in tears because they were so grateful." Gloria said, while trying to smile through the tears.

"Yeah, it was really kind and generous of you guys to do this. I know things have been quiet on our end but it's just been a lot and we have been staying at Gloria's parents since we got back. Hopefully after the memorial things start to get back to a somewhat normal state." Steven said as he glanced over at Gloria.

She smiled at him for a moment and then looked over at her parents as they made their way to stand next to the headstone. Gloria glanced over at Steven and they began to walk in the same direction. As they approached the headstone, Steven and Gloria stood next to her parents. The parents began the memorial and was followed up by the family's priest. When it came time for Gloria's part of the memorial Steven was right by her side.

Both Chuck and Christy were in tears for most of the memorial but when Gloria read what she had written for Harper, Christy couldn't control her emotions. The tears went from a slow pace to consistently streaming down Christy's face. Chuck wiped away the tears rolling down his face and handed Christy some tissues that he had put in his jacket before they left home. He put his arm around Christy's shoulders, gave her a gentle squeeze and kissed the side of her head. Christy placed one arm around his lower back, her other hand on his chest and rested her head on the front of his shoulder.

They stood that way for the rest of the memorial. Once the memorial ended Chuck and Christy walked over to where Gloria and Steven were standing. After a few minutes of silence, Christy spoke first.

“That poem you wrote was beautiful Gloria, Harper would have loved it. The whole ceremony was really beautiful.” Said Christy.

“Yes, such a great turn out and your poem was amazing.” Chuck added to Christy's comment.

“Thank you both. It wouldn’t have been possible without you guys. I mean we would have had a memorial but it might have been a few months later instead of today.” Said Gloria to Chuck and Christy.

Steven had seen that Chuck kept glancing over at someone standing off to their side. “Everything OK Cuz?” Steven asked him.

“Does anyone know that guy?” Chuck asked the group.

They all responded “No” in unison.

“He seems a bit odd just standing there.” Christy said. “Do you guys want to grab a bite to eat?” She asked.

"I'm not very hungry. Haven't really had much of an appetite lately. I know it'll get easier with time but I kinda just want to go lay down." Gloria said as she held on to Stevens arm.

"Maybe another time then. We are here for you guys if you need anything." Chuck said to Steven and Gloria.

"We know cuz and we appreciate it. Today was just a lot to deal with. We're gonna get going but I'll text ya later." Steven said as he hugged Chuck before he and Gloria began walking to Stevens' vehicle.

Chuck and Christy stayed for a moment to say their goodbye to Harper and to get a better look at the headstone.

"Was this our fault? I mean was there any way that we could have prevented Harper from dying?" She asked with a solemn look on her face.

"The only way this could have been avoided or prevented was if we never left for the island. But who's to say that Chloe wouldn't have found us somewhere else. She was set on getting her revenge and one way or another she would have gotten it. If anything, this is my fault and no one else's. She wanted me, so if I would have just given her what she wanted then maybe Harper would be here instead of me." Chuck looked down at his feet and tried his best to hold the tears back, he failed as one rolled down his cheek falling onto his shoe.

"So, sadly, either way someone would have died because I wasn't about to give you up without a fight. I'm sorry I asked you that question Chuck. Let's go home." Christy said as she kissed his cheek..

As they were walking to their vehicles, Chuck noticed that the stranger had left. He looked around for him because he never heard a car start or drive away. He shrugged off the curiosity and opened the door for Christy. She paused before getting into the passenger seat of his Bronco and looked at him. Chuck had that same spine tingling stare that he did when they first pulled into the cemetery.

"What's wrong? You have that same look from earlier and before." Christy nervously asked Chuck.

"I don't know but there was something about the guy that was just standing in the distance and watching us." He replied.

"The one claiming to be an old manager of Harpers?" She asked him.

"Yeah. I don't think he was telling the truth. There was something seriously off about him and it's giving me a bad feeling." Said Chuck with a nervous tone in his voice.

Christy looked at him with concern. “What kind of bad feeling are we talking about? Like the island kind of bad feeling or just a creepy bad feeling?” She asked with a tremble in her voice.

“Honestly, I'm not sure. There is something in my gut telling me that this guy is bad news.” Chuck replied.

“Should we tell Gloria and Steven?” Christy asked.

“NO!” He replied loudly. “I don't wanna give them any more reason to avoid us. Plus, I don't know anything for sure, it's just a bad feeling. They're still distant with us and I'd like to fix that before I start making any crazy accusations.”

“I get that and it makes sense.” Christy said to Chuck and then pointed forward. “Steven is waiving to you.”

Chuck waived back to his cousin and they made their way home. The entire ride home was quiet. He could shake the feeling that the supposed manager was someone far more dangerous. He was finally distracted when Christy giggled while looking at her phone. “What up?” He asked her.

“Gloria just texted me asking if we wanted to grab dinner sometime next week.” Christy said excitedly.

“Hey. That's great news. I'm down for whatever day you guys decide on.” He replied smiling.

“Umm… How about Thursday around seven in the evening?” Christy asked Chuck as he was driving them home.

“Yeah, that works for me.” Chuck replied to her. “Where are we thinking about having dinner?” There is that hibachi place that just opened up, been seeing some good reviews about the place online.” Chuck suggested.

“Ooo yeah, that's a good idea. I’ll ask if that will work for them.” Said Christy.

She quickly messaged Gloria, “Hey, what do you guys think about that new hibachi place that just opened up? Chuck has been seeing some good reviews for that place.”

After a few minutes Gloria replied with a smiley face and thumbs up emoji. “Steve said he was hearing good things about it too.”

Christy texted her back, “We’re looking forward to seeing you guys. We miss you both.”

“We miss you guys too. It’ll be good to get back to some sense of normalcy. Things have just been so depressing and sad lately. This week needs to go by quickly.” Responded Gloria.

Christy texts her back. "I agree. Normal would be nice. I'll text ya later, we are about to grab some dinner before we head home. Love ya Glo."

"Love ya too. We'll chat soon." Gloria replied back to Christy.

"Ok. We are all set for Thursday. I am so happy that we all will finally get together. I think we really need this so we can move forward and get things back to where they need to be." Christy said to Chuck as he pulled into the parking lot of Mission BBQ.

"Is this OK?" He asked Christy.

"Yeah babe, you know I like this place. Just one small request, can we take it to-go and eat at home?" She said, smiling at him.

"No problemo, my love." Chuck replied cheerfully.

They went in, ordered their food and got back in the car to head home for a quiet meal. When they got home, Chuck had grabbed their mail from the box and carried it up with the food. On the way to the kitchen, he threw the mail onto the table to the left of the door and walked over to the dining room table. He turned on spotify and they listened to some music while they ate. Every so often he would make a funny face at Christy while they ate, one of the times she laughed too hard and a piece of a noodle shot out of her nose. They both laughed so hard that tears were rolling down their cheeks.

The following week flew by as they had hoped and it was finally Thursday. Chuck and Christy were getting ready to meet up with Steven and Gloria when his phone rang. He pulled his phone out of his back pocket and checked the caller ID. When he looked at the screen, his whole body froze and in what felt like a slow motion movie reel, he dropped his phone. Christy looked over to him to see why he had dropped his phone. He was as pale as a ghost and she could see a look of bone chilling fear on his face.

"Who was it?" She asked him hesitantly.

"The caller ID said unknown. The last time I received something from an unknown number was before the trip to the island." He said as he stared at his phone on the floor. He was reluctant to pick it up but knew he couldn't just leave it there forever. So, he knelt down, slowly picked up the phone and looked at the screen. There was a voicemail notification on the screen, he pushed it and listened to the message. After a brief moment, his expression softened and he began laughing hysterically. He looked over at Christy, who was looking at him with confusion. “Do you want to extend the warranty on your 2005 Pontiac G6?” He said as he began laughing again.

Christy burst out laughing and even snorted from laughing so hard. “Sir, you scared the ever loving shit out of me and all because of a damn car warranty marketing call. Holy crap Chuck. I need a drink.” She said to him as she shook her head and chuckled.

“You and me both. That was just ridiculous, I'm so sorry babe. I don’t know why I reacted that way. I mean I know why but I shouldn't have. I guess I have some PTSD when it comes to unknown callers.” He chuckled at how crazy that sounded.

“I get it, I really do, but she’s dead and gone now. We don’t have anything to worry about anymore. Things are going to get better and eventually all those lingering fears will fade away.” She grabbed his face and kissed him on the forehead.

“And here I thought it was my job to comfort you and tell you that everything was going to be ok.” He smiled at her. “I know it’ll just take some time to mentally get back to normal, until then I have Dr. Christy taking care of me.” Chuck pulled her close to him and kissed her.

“I’ll be sure to send you the bill for my therapy sessions and services.” She gave him a mischievous smile as she gave him a slow passionate kiss.

“Wow, it just hot in here.” Chuck’s face had turned red from blushing. “Maybe we better get going or I have a feeling we may not make it to the restaurant.” Chuck said as every inch of his body wanted to skip dinner and stay home with Christy.

“You are probably right. Ok, let's get moving.” Christy said to him.

They left the apartment and climbed into Chuck's Bronco. They were only a few minutes away from the apartment when Chuck noticed a black car following them. The other car had matched his every turn and was keeping its distance from his Bronco. Chuck was watching his rearview mirror so much that he was startled when Christy yelled at him.

“Hey. Watch your speed. You're doing eighty-five and we’re in a fifty-five mile per hour zone. Are you trying to get us pulled over?” Christy said to him with an irritated tone.

“What? No. Sorry. I thought I saw something in the rearview mirror and didn’t even notice that I had been speeding up.” Chuck said to her. He felt embarrassed that he didn't notice he was speeding up, but when he looked in his mirror again the black car was gone. He was beginning to wonder if his paranoia was getting the best of him.

Christy was about to ask him what he thought he saw but he made a turn and the restaurant was now in sight. She quickly text Gloria that they were about to pull into the parking lot. She looked at Chuck with concern but decided to keep her thoughts to herself until they got home after dinner. She wanted tonight to be relaxing and fun, not drama filled and annoying.

As they walked into the restaurant they saw Gloria and Steven sitting in the chairs at one of the hibachi tables. They waved to them and made their way over. They gave each other hugs and Chuck gave Steven a half hug handshake. Christy sat next to Gloria and Chuck sat on the opposite side of Christy. They noticed that both Gloria and Steven were smiling and had a look like they were holding a surprise in.

"Whats going on?" Christy asked them. "You guys look extremely happy and suspicious at the same time."

"Is it that obvious?" Gloria asked with a giggle. "We have some big news to share with you guys." Gloria looked over at Steven with a smile bigger than a kid's on Christmas morning.

“Well don't keep us in suspense, what's the news?” Chuck asked.

Gloria held out her left hand and wiggled her fingers. “We're engaged!” She exclaimed with pure joy.

“Oh my god, congratulations guys. I am so happy for you two” Christy said with a high pitched excited voice. She stood up, hugged Gloria tightly and then hugged Steven just as much.

“Wow, that's so great. Congrats guys.” Chuck said smiling and getting up to hug his cousin and then Gloria.

“Thank you. I am so happy.” Gloria said with tears of joy in her eyes. “Steve asked me when we got back to his place after Harper's memorial. It was so sweet and romantic.” She said while looking at her fiancé.

“Well, I guess that makes this dinner a celebration dinner.” Chuck said as he flagged down a server and ordered a bottle of champagne.

Gloria went into the details of how Steven proposed and never once did she stop smiling. She kept looking at her gorgeous ring and at Steven. “He completely caught me off guard but I can't wait to marry him. My sweet romantic fiancé.” She leaned over and kissed Steven who was just enjoying watching her smile and telling them the story.

“That's just amazing.” Chuck said as he raised his champagne glass. “A toast to our newly engaged friends. May you both have a happy life together filled with love, laughter and so many great memories together.” They clinked their glasses together and sipped their champagne.

The night went by amazingly. They chatted about work and living together. Gloria talked about the wedding and possible honeymoon ideas. Gloria even asked Christy to be her Maid of Honor, which of course she accepted. There were so many laughs that it felt like old times, before the island.

“Ladies, if you'll excuse us, I need to borrow my cousin.” Steven said as he nodded for Chuck to follow him.

They went over to the bar, which was at the opposite end of the restaurant. Steven ordered Chuck a beer and one for himself. They took a couple sips in silence and then Steven looked at his cousin.

“Uh, what's up?” Chuck asked him nervously.

“I need to say something to you and I need to ask you to let me finish before you say anything.” Steven said with a serious look on his face.

“Ok, yeah. I'm all ears.” Chuck replied.

“Ok.” Steven took a deep breath, held it in for a moment and then exhaled. “When we first got back from the island, I was pissed at you. I blamed you for everything that happened to us and especially for Harper." Steven could see the smile on Chuck's face quickly disappearing. "The more I dwelled on it, the more I blamed you. Then you paid for the headstone and I thought you were just trying to buy our forgiveness." He took a sip of his beer and continued. "One night, while I was trying to fall asleep it hit me, it was like a moment of clarity. You were, in your own way, trying to protect us. You tried to keep us at a distance in order to keep us safe but you really had no control of the situation. Hell, even if you tried to tell us, we probably wouldn't have believed you. That day, in the bathroom of the gas station, I saw something that I could not believe and you were able to make me think that I imagined it. I saw you, an older or more weathered version of you but it was you. It was the version of you that we saw in that photo in the restaurant. You tried to tell us about it and what was going on but none of us believed it."

Chuck took a swig of his beer and looked at his cousin. As much as he tried he could not hold back the tears that rolled down his face.

"I realized that night that I was blaming the wrong person. I put all this energy into being so angry that I was blinded by it, until that moment. I'm so sorry Chuck. I should have been there for you, like family is supposed to do but I wasn't. That will never happen again. If you ever need me, I am there. I have your back cuz and I hope you'll have mine at the wedding. I want you to be my best man. There is no one on this earth that I can think of that I want to be standing up there with me as I marry Gloria." Steven stopped to give Chuck a moment to take all of what he said in.

"I blamed myself too. Honestly, I still do but Christy keeps reminding me otherwise." Chuck took a second, he looked down and then at his cousin. "I would be honored and proud to be your best man Steven." He smiled and hugged his cousin, who hugged him right back.

They finished their beers and went back to the table with the girls. They looked at them both suspiciously and then at each other with confusion. "Is everything ok with you two?" Christy asked before Gloria could.

Chuck smiled. "Everything is great. You're looking at the future groom and his best man."

Christy and Gloria shrieked with excitement and joy. "This is definitely a great night. I love you guys so much." Christy said as she looked around at her friends.

Once they all finished dinner and boxed up their leftovers, Chuck grabbed the bill to pay before anyone else could get a chance. He walked up to the cashier, handed her the check and his credit card.

"How was everything sir?" The young woman asked him.

"It was amazing, thank you. One of the best nights of my life to be exact." Chuck bragged.

"That is wonderful to hear. So, it looks like your bill was already taken care of, there was even a generous tip left for the staff. We hope to see you back soon."

"What do you mean it was already taken care of? I grabbed the check before anyone else at the table. Do you know who paid for it?" Chuck asked her with some shock and confusion in his voice.

"I'm sorry sir, the person who paid wished to do so anonymously." She replied.

"Wow. Ok. Well, thank you and thanks to whomever paid our bill." Chuck said as he walked away still confused as to who would pay their bill.

He got back to the table and everyone could see the confusion on his face. "Someone paid the bill already." He said to them, "Did one of you guys prepay or something?" He asked.

Gloria, Steven and Christy all replied "No" at the same time.

“Well, whoever it was even left the tip and asked to remain anonymous.” Chuck said as he looked at each of them.

“Maybe someone overheard the good news and decided to celebrate with us by paying the bill.” Christy said, trying to help Chuck make some sense of the surprise.

“Yeah. That's a good possibility. We weren't exactly quiet about it.” Gloria said, chuckling.

“True. I think it's safe to say that we had a really really good night then.” Chuck said smiling. “Amazing news and great food that was all free. Do you guys wanna go grab a drink somewhere?”

“Maybe next time, I don’t know about you guys but I have to work tomorrow morning.” Said Gloria.

“Ok. Definitely next time.” Chuck said with a smile. “I missed you guys.”

“We missed you guys too. I am glad we were able to get together.” Steven said as he and Gloria gave Chuck and Christy hugs goodbye.

While they were all walking out of the restaurant Chuck's phone rang and said “UNKNOWN CALLER.” He looked at it nervously but decided to just hit the red end call button. As he was about to put his phone back into his back pocket it buzzed and the screen showed that he had a voicemail. He swiped it away assuming it was just another annoying sales call. They got into his Bronco and began driving home.

“Another telemarketer?” Christy asked him.

“Yeah, probably. Didn’t feel like wasting my time listening to the robot try and extend my non-exsistent car warranty of the voicemail for it.” Chuck said snickering.

They got home and Chuck had to use the bathroom. As he was sitting on the toilet he began scrolling through his social media, as most guys do when they’re on the throne, the voicemail notification popped back up. He let out an annoyed sigh and pressed the notification icon. The phone dialed up his voicemail account. When the message began playing Chuck was confused because there was nothing but silence. Maybe the robot responses didn’t kick in when the voicemail picked up. He deleted the message and went back to scrolling through random videos. He sent a few love themed clips to Christy and then finished up in the bathroom. When he made it to the bedroom, Christy looked up at him and smiled.

“I thought maybe you fell in or got lost. I was about to send a search party to come find you.” Christy joked.

“Ha ha. I played the voicemail from that unknown number but there was nothing there. It was just silence.”

Chuck said to her as he started putting on some comfy pj pants.

"That's weird but not like you were gonna buy whatever they were selling anyways." She replied back to him.

"True. What ya wanna watch? I picked last time, I think it was *Gremlins*." Chuck said as he passed Christy the remote.

"Ugh. I don't wanna pick. You can put on whatever you wanna watch." Christy replied as she snuggled up to Chuck.

Chuck flipped through movies on Netflix and decided on a movie called *Better Watch Out.* About half way through the movie Christy fell asleep. Chuck smiled and continued watching the movie. When it ended he gently woke Christy up and walked her to bed. As he climbed into bed his phone rang again, but this time when he looked at the screen the name he saw on the caller ID, chilled him to his core. It was Harper's name that appeared on the caller ID. With intense fear and anger, he answered the phone.

"Hello!" He answered with a sharp tone in his voice.

There was no response.

“Who is this and why are you calling from this number.” His voice got louder and meaner, he even woke up Christy with his tone.

She was still half asleep and confused when she asked him, "What's going on?” She could see the look of anger and hurt on his face.

“WHO IS THIS?” He demanded. The only thing he heard was a low raspy growl. He turned up the volume and he could hear a very low voice that was practically a mumble. As he listened to it longer, trying to make out the words, he began to feel dizzy and light headed. Chuck stood up, took a couple steps and collapsed to the ground. He dropped his phone and was barely able to catch himself. Landing on his hands and knees, he looked up at Christy as the call ended. “The caller ID said Harper.” He said as he shakily made his way to his feet.

“Huh? What do you mean it said Harper?” Christy asked Chuck with tears in her eyes.

He held out his phone, with the recent call list on the screen to show her that the caller ID actually said Harper. Now that he was feeling a bit more steady, he walked over to the bed and sat across from Christy. He could see the storm of emotions that was brewing inside of her. He reached out and grabbed her hand. “Maybe the phone company reassigned her number?" He said trying to make sense of the whole situation.

"No, the phone was destroyed when she died. Gloria had to get access to her email in order to get the photos, videos and stuff that was saved on the phone. The only way that anyone could be calling from her number is if they cloned the sim card or they had the original phone repaired. It just doesn't make any sense, why would someone do that?" Christy said angrily.

"I don't know, there wasn't anyone around that day, just us. Unless she dropped it in the cave when Chloe… when she was attacked." Chuck was struggling to make sense of what was going on.

"You don't think there is any possible way either Chloe or Harper survived, do you?" Christy asked Chuck with fear in her voice.

"No, I don't think so. If Chloe would have survived then I'm pretty sure we would have seen her by now. Plus, I seriously doubt that she would leave me alive, especially with the element of surprise on her side. Harper was literally a pile of ashes so there is absolutely no way possible she survived what happened." Chuck said with certainty in his voice.

“Then either someone is playing a very cruel joke or there is something else going on.” Christy said with some irritation in her voice.

“Something in my gut tells me it's something else and that scares the crap out of me. After everything that we have been through, I can’t imagine anything worse than what's already happened.” Chuck sighed with exhaustion.

“I hate to do this but I think we should call Gloria and Steven. Maybe they got calls too. If there is something going on, we all need to be on the same page.” Her voice was sounding more frantic than usual.

“I don’t know babe. If it was just a freak coincidence then we risk pushing them away and having them be pissed at us. I don't want to jump the gun before we know anything for sure, you know what I mean?” He said to Christy with a mix of feelings. His mind was racing with the what ifs, again, and he hoped and prayed that it was just something simple. Though, in the pit of his stomach, there was an uneasy feeling.

“I get what you're saying but I think they should know about the call. Even if it was just something like the phone company reassigning the number. I don’t want there to be any secrets or anything like that with our little group.” Christy said with conviction.

“Ok, but just give me a day to try and figure out what or who called from her number.” Chuck said with hope that he would be able to prove that it was just a coincidence.

“One day, that's all.” Christy reluctantly agreed.

“Peferct. Thank you.” He said with a smile.

Chuck was already trying to find a website to do a reverse search on the number to see if maybe it would give an estimated location of the caller. Unfortunately, all he got was the current owner's name, which was Harper. He knew the best way to try to get a last known location would be by getting into her online account and without talking to Gloria, that wasn’t going to happen. His next idea was to call the number and see if anyone picked up. This idea made him nervous because if someone did answer, he wasn't sure if the results would be good or bad. He looked over at Christy, who was already fast asleep, and decided to go into the living room and call the number.

He stared at her name for a bit before he worked up the nerve to hit the dial icon. With a weary sigh he called Harper's number. He listened to it ring several times before her voicemail picked up. Tears began rolling down his cheeks as he listened to her voice. It was the first time he heard it since that day on the beach, the day that she died.

When the voicemail recording ended he heard the beep to leave a message.

“Harper, I am so sorry. I wish things would have gone differently and I was the one who had died that day instead of you. You didn’t deserve any of that, none of you did. I miss you my friend. I love you Harper. Good-bye.” Chuck ended the call and a tear rolled off of his face and landed on the phone's screen.

Just when he stood up to go back to bed, the phone rang. He looked down at the screen with fear and hesitation. It was Harper’s name on the caller ID. Chuck's hands started to shake as he looked at his phone. When he answered the phone, his blood ran ice cold.

“Chuck? Is that really you?” Is what he heard, in his dead friend's voice.

“H.. Harper? Yes it's me but how are you alive?” Chuck's voice was trembling with fear.

“I’m not, I’m dead. I’m dead and it's all because of you. It is your fault that I am dead, it's your fault that my family had to have a memorial for me and that my sister is all alone. Are you happy with yourself?” The more she talked the raspier her voice became.

“No, it’s not my fault Harper. I tried to protect you guys from the monster. Please, I need you to know that. I never wanted any of this to happen." Chuck said with pain in his voice.

"No, Chuck. You are the monster. You got me killed, you got Jacob killed and almost got everyone else killed too." Her voice became deeper.

"This isn't Harper. Who is this?" Chuck realized that Harper never knew about Jacob. No one but him and Christy knew about him.

In a deep, rumbling and menacing tone, Harper's voice was replaced by a man's voice. "You took something from me. Something that can never be replaced. Soon you will know my pain and you will feel it ten fold."

Chuck tried to hang up the phone but he became very dizzy and lightheaded. The room felt as if it was spinning. With each step he took the room spun faster and faster until he finally fell over. He tried to grab the table in front of him but instead knocked over a chair. He hit the left side of his head on the leg of the chair before completely blacking out as he hit the ground.

Christy woke up to a loud sound from outside of the bedroom. "Chuck." She waited but got no response. "Chuck are you out there?" She called out from the bed. She slid out of the bed slowly and made her way to where she heard the loud noise. "Chuck!" She screamed out as she saw him lying on the floor. As she ran over to his side she could see a small pool of blood on the hardwood floor from where he hit his head. She immediately called 911.

While she had them on speaker phone she texted Gloria and Steven that they were about to be heading to the ER. She told them how she found Chuck unconscious and bleeding from the side of his head. Once the paramedics arrived she told them what she knew, they loaded him onto the stretcher and rushed him to their rig. They turned on the sirens and sped all the way to the hospital. Gloria texted her that they would meet her there.

The whole scene was chaotic as doctors and nurses surrounded him on the hospital bed. They hooked him up to machines, they ran scans and did blood work on him. Christy felt helpless as she sat in the waiting room with Gloria and Steven. She would get up and pace then sit down for a few moments then get up again and pace around the waiting room.

“Christy, come sit down. Pacing and worrying yourself so much isn't doing you any good. Please come sit with us.” Gloria pleaded with her.

“I can't just sit there Glo. I'm freaking out and I can't do anything to help him. I should have been up with him or made him come to bed. I should never have left him alone. Not after that call." Christy said with tears rolling down her face

"What call?" Steven asked her.

Christy looked at them both and collapsed in the chair next to them. "He got a call and the caller ID had Harper's name on it."

"What? What do you mean it had her name on it? That's impossible." Gloria said in disbelief.

"It did. I saw the caller ID. He wanted to investigate it before we told you guys. We were hoping that it was just something simple like the number being reassigned. When I laid back down he was looking up stuff to try and figure it out. He was afraid that if we told you tonight it would push you guys away or piss you both off." Her tone had gone monotone and she was feeling mentally exhausted.

"I can appreciate his concern but that wouldn't have pushed us away. We are a family and we are and will stick together." Steven said to Christy in a reassuring tone.

"Thank you both. That means so much to me. To us both." She said with relief in her voice.

They all looked up as the ER doctor came walking towards them. "Are you the family for Mr. Jones?" He said looking at all of them.

In unison they stood up and said yes.

"Ok. At the moment we are currently monitoring him. His vitals are all stable, the scans and blood work came back normal. There is no medical reason that we can find to explain his current situation." Said the doctor.

"So, he's just in a coma and you have no idea why? How did that make any sense? You guys need to do more. Run more tests. There has to be something wise you can do." Steven barked at the doctor.

"Sir, I understand your frustration and please believe me when I say that we are doing anything and everything we possibly can." The doctor said sympathetically. "If you'd like, I can take you to his room so you all can see him."

"Steven, calm down please. And yes doctor. Please take us to his room." Christy said.

The doctor led them to Chuck's room. They were surprised to see him lying there with a tube down his throat. He had on an oxygen mask and the monitors were steadily beeping. Christy walked over to Chuck, grabbed his hand and kissed his forehead where they had bandaged his wound. She sat down and began crying.

Gloria walked over to her and hugged her. "He looks good, Christy. Peaceful and comfortable."

Gloria watched Steven walk up to his cousin and put a hand on his shoulder. "Hey cuz. We are here with you. Come back to us." Steven said as he held back tears.

Three hours had passed when Christy looked at Gloria and Steven as they slept on the small couch in the room. "You guys can go, if you want. Go home and get some rest. I'll be here with him." Christy herself was getting tired too.

"Are you sure sweetie?" Gloria said.

"Yeah. I'll be fine here. Come back tomorrow after you get some sleep." Christy said then yawned.

"OK. Try to get some sleep. We'll be back in the morning with coffee and breakfast." Steven said as he kissed her on the top of her head.

As they left Chuck's room and made their way to the parking garage they walked in silence. Steven was the one to break that silence. "What the hell is going on Glo?"

"I was wondering the same thing. Why would someone be calling him with Harper's number and how? I don't like this Steve, it scares me." Gloria said to Steven.

"Me too babe. Me too." Steven said as he opened her door to get in the vehicle.

Chuck was feeling the pain in his head from his fall. He started groaning in bed and he opened his eyes. He could hear someone calling for the nurse saying he was walking up. As he opened his eyes, he looked at both sides of the room. He wondered where Christy was or even Gloria or Steven.

"Hello Mr. Jones. How are you feeling?" Said a man in a white coat.

Chuck looked up at him and blinked a couple of times. "My head hurts." He said.

"I'm sure it does, you one heck of a fall." The doctor replied. "Can you follow my finger with your eyes only?" He asked as he moved his finger left to right and up then down.

Chuck did as he was asked. "Who are you?" Chuck asked the doctor.

"Ah, sorry. Forgot my manners in my office. My name is Dr. Rowan. Do you know where you are, Mr. Jones?" Dr. Rowan asked him.

"Well, if you're a doctor then I must be in the hospital. And call me Chuck please." He said to Dr. Rowan.

"Very good. Very good." Said Dr. Rowan.

"Where is Christy?" Chuck asked.

"Umm… I don't think nurse Christy works today. I believe nurse Chloe and Harper are here today. Would you like me to call them? Did you need something?" Replied the doctor.

"What? Christy, my girlfriend. Where is she?" Chuck asked with confusion.

"Maybe you hit your head harder than we thought. Chuck, what hospital do you think you're at?" Dr. Rowan asked with concern in his voice.

"I don't know. We were home and I had a weird phone call then I fell and woke up here. So, I guess whatever ER the ambulance brought me to." Chuck said with some irritation in his voice.

"Chuck. You are in a psychiatric hospital and you have been here for about a month. You fell last night and got your head on the bathroom sink. Another patient by the name of Christy found you on the floor in your bathroom in a puddle of blood. Perhaps we should do another scan of your head." Dr. Rowan said to Chuck.

"What the hell are you talking about? I have never been to a psychiatric hospital and I'm not in one now. This is not a funny joke." Chuck said as he tried to sit up. He stopped when he realized he was in restraints and was stuck in bed.

"Whoa. Slow down there Chuck. You were sent here about a month ago after you were in a car crash. After the accident you became quite delusional and paranoid thinking you were being followed. Once you came to us, you said that a vampire was trying to kill you because of something that happened in a past life. You even brought staff and other patients into your story." Dr. Rowan spoke to Chuck in a soft and gentle tone.

"Did my cousin Steven put you up to this? Is he trying to top my pranks because this is pretty good. So how about you let me out of these restraints and we give him his props." Chuck said to the doctor.

"This is no prank nor is it a joking matter. You are a patient here and we have been working together for a while now. I fear that your fall has set you back drastically. It appears you've had a full relapse and we are going to have to either increase your medications or begin something much more intense. Also, Steven is not your cousin but a CNA that works here, he is one of our best employees. He is actually out here, sitting in the milieu with the other patients. If you agree to be calm and cooperative, I can undo the restraints and bring you out with the other patients." Dr. Rowan said to Chuck as he moved slowly over to the restraints on his hands.

"Yes, I will be calm and cooperative. I shouldn't even be here but I am not a violent person." Chuck replied with irritation in his voice.

"When you first got here, you were quite aggressive and you did injure one of the techs who was bringing you a meal tray. You made great improvements and your recovery has been remarkable. That's why it pains me to see you set so far back from where you were. However, I am going to take your word and I will remove the restraints." Said the doctor as he freed Chuck's right arm.

"Thanks Doc." Chuck said as he sat up and rubbed his wrists. "So, what do I have to do to get out of here? Take my meds, play nice with the staff and patients and join in when they have groups?" Chuck asked him. Chuck had a friend who worked at a psych hospital and that what she always said was needed to get discharged from a place like that.

"Well, that and your discharge is at my discretion. We need to see and believe that you are truly getting better and being truthful with us about your progress. Only then can we consider discharging you." Dr. Rowan said to Chuck as they made their way to the milieu.

As they walked down the hall Chuck noticed photographs on the walls of past staff members. The further they walked the more recent the photos were. When Chuck got to the current year, he stopped dead in his tracks. In the photo he saw several familiar faces and they were listed with job titles. RN Cassandra, LPN Chloe, CNA Steven, CNA Harper, and Activity Therapist Gloria. Chuck could not believe what he was seeing, everyone that had been in his dreams and with him on the island were listed in that picture. He even saw the other patient that he knew as his cousin Steven, sitting at a table in the milieu reading a book.

The only words that Chuck could get out were, "What the hell is going on."

www.ingramcontent.com/pod-product-compliance
Lightning Source LLC
LaVergne TN
LVHW041012150826
845672LV00001B/60

* 9 7 9 8 9 9 5 0 9 8 3 2 4 *